D0445242

BY
ANY MEANS
NECESSARY

BY ANY MEANS NECESSARY

CANDICE MONTGOMERY

PAGE STREET
PUBLISHING CO.

PAGE STREET
PUBLISHING CO.

Copyright © 2019 Candice Montgomery

First published in 2019 by
Page Street Publishing Co.
27 Congress Street, Suite 105
Salem, MA 01970
www.pagestreetpublishing.com

Distributed by Macmillan, sales in Canada by The Canadian Manda Group.

23   22   21   20   19   1   2   3   4   5

ISBN-13: 978-1-62414-799-9
ISBN-10: 1-62414-799-9

Library of Congress Control Number: 2019933280

Cover and book design by Laura Gallant for Page Street Publishing Co.
Author photo by McKaylyn Barth Photography
Photograph of boy © iStock / m-imagephotography; painting of cityscape
© Shutterstock / anna42f; emojis © Shutterstock

Printed and bound in the United States

FOR MY GRAMMA HONEY.
I LOVE YOU.
THAT CHIPPENDALES CRUISE
IS STILL WAITING FOR US.
XO, KITTEN

*T*here is a special kind of hell for people who wait to open their official-looking mail. People like me.

It's not my fault.

Can I say that?

Shake the blame, here? It's the way my aunt Lisa always operates. Having her in my life for seventeen years has ingrained in me a long habit of avoiding bill collectors, debt companies, delinquent hospital bills, and Girl Scouts.

Those cute little assholes will finesse you for $50 and ten boxes of Thin Mints before you can blink twice. The Girl Scouts, not the debt collectors.

I like to call this horrific habit a symptom of "Poverty PTSD." (I won't trademark that, you're welcome, have at it.) The avoidance, not the addiction to waxy, chocolate-mint cookies.

Comes from being broke all the time, from being a Black kid constantly screwed over by the system, unable to catch a break, from hearing your uncle's been gunned down by the police for no discernible reason.

So, here we are. Jump cut to me, standing just over the threshold of my new home, my new dorm room at college, duffel heavy on my back, phone to my head as my auntie Lisa yells in my ear.

"Torrey, did you hear what I just said?"

Yes, but my brain's, like, waiting for a jump start or something, and my dumbass doesn't own jumper cables. I also suddenly have to pee, but I don't think I passed a men's bathroom on the way up.

Lisa, my aunt by marriage, is the one in charge. I put things in her hands as I left for what I naively thought was my way out. My one and probably only chance to walk away from the thin strings holding me to the shreds of my sad excuse for a family. But this, my bees: I trusted her to handle this, and I don't know how things have already fallen apart.

I laid everything out. I put the entire operation on a silver platter and said, *Here, Auntie, bees, simplicity, money—all you.* She isn't the best at organization. But she's smart. Capable. A scientist, even!

But I should've expected it, you know? The neighborhood doesn't just let you walk. It doesn't just let you out sans so much as an ass scratch or a backward glance.

"Torr. Listen to me." And then she enunciates, which is probably a good thing. "This letter is talking about shutting down and selling the apiary."

Even though I just dropped my bags, I say, "I'm coming home." Calling it home is such a farce. *Home* is a safe haven. Baldwin Hills is a place I reside.

"What? No. You're not. There's no reason for you to come home. Yet."

Then why the hell would she call me with this letter, all panicked? "Where are you? Where's Theo?"

"I'm at Theo's now."

"So he knows? What's he saying?"

For a second there's some shuffling on her end of the line and it prompts me to walk fully inside the dorm room. It's a double. Not huge but big enough for at least (and at most) two people to breathe in at the same time.

Aunt Lisa exhales slowly. She mostly does this for me, to help regulate my breathing. "Well. You know Theo, baby."

I am very self-actualized. Self-actualized enough that I understand that Lisa is my stand-in for maternal comfort and has been for a while now. She doesn't have any kids of her own. And she's only, like, a decade older than me. But still. She's all I got anymore. And all I want, really. My high school counselor used to say I was lying to myself about wanting more because I never got a "real mom," whatever that is, and I guess I'm supposed to feel cheated out of that? But like I said, I'm self-actualized. And Lisa's enough.

"Titi. Can they really do that?" I ask. *Titi.* Kinda funny, isn't it? How universal the nickname is. It's a term all Black kids grow up knowing their favorite auntie as.

Her voice gets thick, and I can see in my head, clear as day, that she's sucking on a cigarette, cherry-red lipstick staining the paper. She didn't start smoking until her husband, my uncle Miles, died.

"I haven't even gotten to make sure you're settling in okay." She's shaking her head right now, I know it. "Technically, yes. They can. The letter states there are unpaid property taxes, and as a result the property is being seized."

"Unpaid property—What? But Theo . . . ?"

"Fell behind. Couldn't catch up."

"Fell behind. That's some bullshit." My back finds the wall and I give in, sliding down into a melted heap of boy on the floor.

"True as that may be, don't you curse at me, boy. I'm not the one."

She really isn't. "I apologize." I know better than to say, "I'm sorry." Not in Black families.

You ain't sorry, boy. You ain't never sorry.

"Mm-hmm," she says. "I understand what you're saying. And I want you to know, Miles never wanted this kind of stress on you. He'd encourage you to save yourself before ever thinking about those bees. But Theo, on the other hand . . ."

4

"Yeah. He never wanted the farm, Titi. You know this. I know this."

Theo only agreed to handle the financial end of things because when Uncle Miles died, he left his bee farm to me, and I was underage at the time. But I'm sure to Theo it felt like a way to keep his son with him. It felt that way to me.

It's what I thought I wanted—owning and running the apiary. I've been working with or learning about bees forever. Working with bees meant working with Uncle Miles. Uncle Miles is—was—the apiary.

It was always just me and Uncle Miles out there, shooting the shit. Talking, commiserating. He met me on his level. Never treated me like a kid who couldn't understand things. Bothered to take the time and teach me things that were new. Bothered to educate me. Bothered to give a shit.

Yeah. Just me and Uncle Miles and the bees. I've loved bees longer than I've loved those frosted brown sugar Pop-Tarts and, for real, that is saying something, I promise you it is. Uncle Miles made sure of that.

But Theo. He never wanted any of this. Thinks the apiary is a waste of space, time, and money. Commonly refers to it as "punk-ass rich shit." So I wouldn't be all that shocked if this nigga fell behind and just decided not to give a single shit about it when things got hot.

Low-key, I feel like I'm about to cry when a deep voice behind me says, "Hey. This is real heavy, could I get some help?"

And just inside my open doorway is Desh. Desharu but Desh.

I recognize his tree trunk of a body and head full of almost too much curly black hair.

Coming to an immediate stand, phone crushed between my shoulder and ear, I grab the largest suitcase from him. It's covered in Sharpie tags, doodles, and different stickers but the largest and most prominent of them all—the ones I catch and can differentiate at a glance—are the two flags. One for Korea. One for India.

Desh reps his people hard. That's no secret; just take a gander at his Facebook reposts.

With his bags "settled" on his side of the room—they aren't settled; they are thrown haphazardly on his bare mattress, his backpack on top of one suitcase, and the larger suitcase I grabbed is the only one that's upright—we sit on our respective mattresses.

"Titi, I gotta go. Lemme call you back." And I hang up before she can yell at me not to. I'mma pay for that later, I already know.

Desh pulls his hoodie off, tosses it into a corner.

When we selected our roommate preferences, I chose the "no preference" option. Meaning, I could wind up with a neat freak or a cyclone of a human, never a thing in place.

I'm somewhere in the middle, so I figured it didn't matter.

Desh is the latter. We've spent the past few weeks DMing about it, among other things. But mostly that Desh has zero plans to clean or organize anything because "you think I'm gonna clean shit when, finally, my mother isn't around to nag me about it?"

I drop my phone on the floor and it makes a nice thud sound. He takes one look at me.

Listen. Here's the thing about Desh.

He doesn't know what personal boundaries are. He doesn't care if asking you about that sore on your lip in polite company is just a smidge too loud. He doesn't care if the way he eats (he doesn't breathe, like, not once during the entire meal does he stop to take a breath) is horrifying and probably a little bit dangerous, he doesn't care if you're not ready to have his Nikon pointed right up in your grill.

Desh doesn't care.

I've learned all this from texts, Facebook messages, and the occasional FaceTime session with him since having been "introduced" two months ago.

And those are the things that make Desh endearing. The loudness, the devil-may-care, the camera that's permanently attached to his hand. Those are the things that make it easy to be friends with him. He's either going to judge you or he's not. But no matter what, he's gonna stick around (and probably photograph it).

Still, even though I like Desh, I don't *know him* know him, when it comes down to it. I'm not the kind of person who's gonna let all my walls down just because you tagged me in some random meme on Facebook once.

I scrub a hand across my head.

Desh clears his throat. "Damn, who died?"

I shake my head. Me. I'm kinda feeling like it's me.

There are a lot of things I need to worry about in life, like, as a Black male teen. A lot of things I have to worry about separately—as a teen and again as a male and then, further still, as a Black person. Confusing, right? Well, try being me. When you combine those separate parts, apparently, I am lethal. I am a problem.

But on the list of things I didn't ever think I'd need to worry about was my safe space being snatched right out of my bony-ass dark fingers by "the city of angels."

Angels my ass. Let me tell you something: There is literally nothing angelic about Los Angeles.

The traffic: bullshit.

The heat: bullshit.

The price to valet: bullshit.

And don't you get me started on the white people moving out to Eagle Rock and Echo Park, and all up in Baldwin Hills.

But this morning I woke up in my room at Theo's like always, heat with its thick-ass fingers wrapped around the back of my neck, and I just felt like something terrible was going to happen. I wake up that way a lot. Anxiety is a straight-up PITA.

Which is why I chalked the feeling up to a case of nerves. Nervous about leaving home, about moving into my dorm, about leaving behind Uncle Miles's and my bees. Nervous about, just, not knowing anything. Being at the bottom again when I spent all of my last year of high school at the figurative top.

Well, here the hell we are now.

Desh stands, pecks around on his phone for a second, then locks it, sliding it into his back pocket.

"You look bad, my guy," he says.

"Not feeling great. So, yeah."

"You going to this freshman-mixer thing?"

Ah. The mixer is supposed to be, like, you get to know the other people in your dorm hall, get to know what the campus has to offer. And I think some of the frats and sororities prowl for fresh meat, too.

"I don't know, man." My head isn't here. It's at the apiary wondering whom I could yell at next for letting things go to shit, for letting go of the space that belongs solely to Uncle Miles and me. It sure as hell isn't Theo. He took me in because there was no other choice.

Ever talk to somebody and literally watch them ignore you? That's Theo. That's Theo all of the time.

Oh, and Theo is my granddad. Theopolis James McKenzie. The name is far more distinguished than the man.

Still, he's the money. Or he was. Was supposed to be "the name on the building." The one whose name is on most of the legal documents where mine couldn't be. He's the man who took care of me when pharmaceutical drugs made my mother believe she couldn't. When the military took my sperm donor to Hawaii and gave him an excuse to never come back, I guess Moms didn't feel like she needed to be present either.

My family keeps doing this thing where they just leave Theo other people he doesn't want. When Moms gave up and went too deep with her prescription love affair, she left Theo me. I like to think that's why Aunt Lisa and I get along so well. We're both Theo's, even though neither of us wants to be and Theo sure as hell doesn't want us either.

When Uncle Miles died, he left his wife, Aunt Lisa, in Theo's care. Not by any legal means. Just . . . Theo's all either of us had after Uncle Miles. So, he became her de facto whatever-the-hell-you-want-to-call-it. I don't know what they are to each other. I guess maybe Aunt Lisa is yet another way for Theo to keep a piece of his son.

And Aunt Lisa . . . She's here because there's nowhere else for her to go. No family on this coast or the other, to speak of.

I reach up to rub the back of my head where my barber nicked my neck a little too close. "I think . . . " I say, then take a deeper inhale than is warranted. I let it go as I continue. "I think I need to head home."

Desh is confused. The look on his face screams pretty solidly, *I am confusion.*

"Okay, why are we going home?" Everything is "we" with Desh. Why are we going home? How are we doing today? I didn't know we had seen every version of the Spider-Man films.

They're not that bad as a franchise goes, don't you think?

"Remember how I told you about my apiary?" I roll my neck. There's a migraine starting somewhere back there, and if I don't curb it now, it's gonna John Cena the hell out of me later.

Stay tuned for that, should it decide to really stick. My chronic migraines are a whole thing. Insert popcorn.gif here.

"Yeah," Desh says. "You and your bee fetish. What about it?"

Bee fetish. "There's some stuff going on with it right now, and it could be really bad. If I'm not there—"

"No," he says. "You're not there."

I glance at him sharply.

"Torrey, you are a billion miles from Los Angeles right now. It's seven o'clock. What the hell kind of superhero shit are you hoping to achieve at this time of night?"

He has a point. SFSU is not a hop-skip-jump from LA. It's

not across the country like Desh's weirdo distance calculation would have you believe, but California is a very large state.

"Here's my plan." Desh always has a plan. "I say we head to this freshman mixer. Mix some of the Absolut that I have in my backpack with whatever sugar-free punch they're serving, scope the party for trade, and just *be here* tonight."

When he can tell I'm about to protest, he says, "Nothing more can fall apart tonight. Nothing can be fixed either. Take the night. You just got here, Torr. Just be here."

I hate when Desh is right. It's rare. But when it happens, it fucking happens.

"Alright. You got me."

"Hell, yeah," he says, offering me a hand to drag my ass up off the cheap excuse for a mattress.

"This is about to sound real dumb, but did you know bees pollinate cotton?" Uncle Miles said. I did know, actually. He'd said it to me once before, right when this whole bee thing started happening for him. Maybe 'bout a year back, just as he'd gotten Miles To Go up and running.

Still, I answered, "Oh, yeah?"

Excited, and on a tear now, he said, "Oh, yeah." The family, his new wife, Aunt Lisa, and even a bunch of people from the neighborhood doubted him when he said the word "apiary" to us. Let's be real, none of us even knew what the hell an apiary was. Uncle Miles, as long as I could remember, had always been adamant about his decision-making, about giving himself the room to think for himself and then feel solid in those decisions and whatever consequence might or might not follow.

"Without bees, we'd be stuck wearing polyester boxer briefs and shit."

"Cotton," I said. I'd had a year to let this percolate, so my delivery was impeccable when I said, bored, "So . . . you like bees for their connection to—"

"Don't make that joke or I'mma have to—"

He was gon' get this joke. "Uncle Miles, they are bee negroes."

"Why do I tell you anything?"

"They're BEEGROES!" I shouted after him as he walked away.

I followed him, so it wasn't hard to miss when he muttered, "Can't take you nowhere."

I take it. Tonight is mine. Some part of my life has got to be mine. Not the apiary's or Mom's or even Lisa and Theo's. Because somewhere along the way, I started taking responsibility for them, too.

"Where's that Absolut at?" I say.

Desh is already lifting the half-full bottle out of his backpack. And somehow, I'm already feeling better.

3.

The mixer is lame as hell. You and I both knew that was gonna be the case, didn't we?

It's a university-run event, so it's pretty much just cheap balloons, cheap foldout chairs, and cheap cheese trays, which really says everything in and of itself.

The whole setup is mostly in Prominski Hall's rec room, which sits at the very bottom floor. I lose Desh within the first five minutes, so I find myself two floors up from that, once again, on my own floor, Floor B. Our entire hallway is littered with people loitering in doorways, cups of something interesting and/or something that tastes like the definition of "toxic" in hand.

Someone's brought out a Bluetooth speaker and is blasting some older Chano tracks all through halls and up against the walls.

I sit right in the threshold of my room and sip on the watery stuff that's in my red Solo cup. Whatever Desh poured and then shoved into my hands . . . yeah, that got disposed of in the nearest drinking fountain. I gave it one sniff, and it made my gums itch.

This threshold is going to be a thing for me. My spot. If I stay here, anyway.

What the hell am I saying? I can't stay. I shouldn't be making future plans in my head like that. I shouldn't be claiming a space, establishing intent, giving it meaning, ready to carve my initials into this proverbial tree. I should be arranging my trip home and figuring out how to square away the other half of the tuition I owe. I should be trying to figure out how to disenroll from my classes. I should be figuring out if "BEES!" is a feasible excuse for a temporary leave of absence. I should—

"Hey, are you Torrey McKenzie?"

I look up from the blue liquid mixture that's in my cup and smile. The first real, genuine one since I got here. I am entirely surprised at how easily it comes, how smoothly my mood shifts.

"Lookit all this CAKE!" I say, standing. The four girls in front of me, introduced to Desh and me by way of the university's student-housing portal, share a suite in the same hall as us. The six of us Skyped a few times, chatted and exchanged numbers eventually. It was a nice way to get comfortable. Ish. To mute the anxiety that comes with new people, new digs, new city, new responsibilities, new credit card, new you-get-the-point.

Still, it's there. The jitters. The first-meeting jitters. Are my eyes open too wide? I don't wanna be smiling all hard with that wild serial-killer look going on.

I guess . . . maybe I'm in the clear, though, because all at once, the four of them—CAKE: Clarke, Auburn, Kennedy, and Emery—wrap me up in what I like to call the "oh, my God!" hug. You know, the one girls do when they're trying to convey their excitement to you in as few words as possible. Mostly I think it's because women know their time is valuable and if they're gonna spend it anywhere, it's not going to be with the likes of me or any other cis college boy.

Especially not these girls. A quad of Black STEM girls? Nope.

The thing is, Black women already fight tooth and nail for what they've got. Add in the fact their interests lie in male-dominated fields—STEM—and then there's an *additional* layer of battling they have to go through.

Totally makes sense that the four of them are no nonsense on every level.

The five of us can't quite fit in the doorway, so as they squeeze through, they move us farther into my room, away from the hum of the other freshmen talking and laughing about their SAT scores just outside the open door.

The girls all talk at me in a collision, grabbing up on my biceps, telling me I shouldn't have shaved my beard off, pretty much reading me the riot act in the same way they do online.

The way they're able to just be *so comfortable* in their skin reminds me of home. Of the Black girls who walk down to the liquor store off 49th, casually friendly with perfect strangers.

I'm not *entirely* sure what STEM cntails, but I know the basics. I get it's some smart-people shit that takes place in spaces usually reserved for the whites.

("The whites." We're going to mention them a lot. Just know I'm not talking about an irritating, neighboring family. "The Whites.")

But that doesn't stop me from *mistaking* STEM for exactly what it isn't every chance I get, just to annoy these four.

"Solve any CSI mysteries on campus yet?" I say, leaning on the bed next to Emery, who is all legs, stretched long and pushed up onto the squat wooden table in the middle of this pseudo group circle.

Auburn bangs her head into the chair back she's seated on. "Torrey," she says with an eye roll.

I mimic her. "Auburn."

Auburn is the epitome of hood. Girl was born and raised in the very (culturally) rich and (no pun intended) riotous beehive of Watts. We were practically neighbors all our lives and didn't even know it. She's all *started from the bottom, now we here.* Don't tell her I used a Drake lyric to talk about her.

"CSI, STEM—not the same thing, honey." That's Clarke. She's the mama bear of the group. There's one in every girl group, they say.

One in every gay group, too. I should know. It was me.

Auburn snorts, says something in Spanish way too fast for my basic ass to catch. "And he knows this."

"Okay, but hear me out—What if it *is* the same?" Kennedy says.

I high-five her because that's my girl. Can always count on her to have my back and irritate the others in her posse with me.

"Exactly," I say.

Clarke rolls her eyes, does this complicated updo thing with her hair. "Glad to see you're just as annoying in person as you are online, Torr."

I laugh as Emery pulls her phone out and watch as her thumb scrolls through some social media app she's only barely paying attention to. "So why aren't you out there?" she says in my direction. "Not interested in this particular socialization tactic?"

"We all know I'm Mr. Sociable, but even this is pushing it for me."

"You always seemed pretty extroverted online." Kennedy shrugs. "Some of the stuff going on in the hallways is pretty cool." This girl. Ever the optimist.

Emery adds, helpfully, "Yeah, there's a girl out there dislocating her shoulder and then popping it back into place."

That gets our collective attention, and for a second we all look up in disgust from our half-hearted social media scrolling.

"How's it going with that girl, Clarke? That horse girl."

"Oh, my God, Torrey, don't call her a horse girl. That's so mean." Clarke's all fluff, too. She just won't ever admit it. "Fine, what's her name again?"

"Rithika. Or River."

I hop over from Twitter to Instagram for the third time in as many minutes. "Her name is River?"

"Shut up," Clarke says. "Your name is Torrey; you're not allowed to talk."

Touché.

There are a couple of new likes on my most recent post, a sneaky Boomerang I snapped of the four of them sitting around my room, faces in phones.

@returnoftheMcKenzie: 👀 📱

One of my three notifications is a new follower.

@leirbagavlis started following you four minutes ago

I have no clue who this is. CAKE continues to chat at and around me, and I'm still listening and responding, but there's like, maybe 12 percent of my attention now being used to figure out who this person is.

Their avi is so small, it's indecipherable. The bolded display name at the top of the private profile is just "gls." But the ratio of followers to following is a reasonable number, so I doubt it's a spam follow.

There is literally no reason for me to be as invested in—and suspicious of—this random follow as I am, save for the fact that maybe it's a few more moments where I can be somewhere else other than back home, thinking about how much fixing I'll have to do this time.

"Torrey, are you listening?" Auburn says.

And it startles me so much that I flub and my thumb hits that stupid fucking FOLLOW BACK button even though I'm still only, like, mid-sleuth, but the universe has other plans, apparently.

I hit home twice. Swipe the app up and closed.

"Shut up, yeah, I'm listening."

Kennedy and Clarke laugh as Auburn tries to reach over them to hit me.

I'm about to ask if they wanna go get food when my phone buzzes and then chimes with a notification that means Instagram. My fingers tap into that app so fast, I'm shocked there isn't permanent damage done to the device.

This time, it's a private DM.

From, yep, you guessed it: @leirbagavlis.

The message reads, *holy shit I found you.*

I hate that I have read receipts running on Insta.

It's the dumbest thing ever. Why do people need to know I've seen their messages? And more importantly, why do they get so peeved if you read the message and then don't respond immediately? I am a person whose time is limited and (kind of) valuable (probably).

Don't rush me.

But in this instance, what's done is done.

I've read the DM and this person knows I've read the DM, and there is literally no reason to worry about it until I know who this person is anyway. This is what I tell myself.

Don't look at me like that, this is a judgment-free zone.

I found you.

Kennedy is asking me if she can borrow the book of poetry that's sticking out of my backpack, some stuff by Mahogany L. Browne. I mumble something to her that I'm pretty sure is a yes, go ahead, but who can know. I'm so busy clicking into this mystery person's profile that I can only really offer a small percentage of my focus outside the realm of my phone and this app now.

Once I'm there, my stomach falls and then jackrabbits up into my throat.

After which, fickle as it is, it begins to dance.

He doesn't have a ton of photos posted. A scant sixty, which isn't really enough for any stranger to form a concrete opinion on. My eyes zero in on the second-to-most-recent image.

And I mean, if you're going to be sparing with Insta post quantity, you had better be ready to plate up some supreme quality.

Somebody give me a green check mark emoji on that one, because wow.

In the photo, he's seated, legs pretzeled, with six very small kittens around and on his lap.

Like, if there were Instagram-post Olympics, he'd take the gold for this one. It's like the world's purest thirst trap.

People love baby animals. People love masc dudes with baby animals. *Unnf, yeah, look at all that muscley forearm and all that feral house cat fur, yes, baby.*

Ridiculous.

It's not the clearest image of his face. But it's enough to spark recognition. The way his chin is tucked down, a secret whispered, lips to heart; eyes closed, a prayer on its own; inky lashes kissing the terra-cotta skin of his cheeks; a smile stretched entirely too far across his face. But his hair. His hair is the giveaway. That particular photo shows it up in this messy ball on the very peak of his head, the kind that I'll never be able to make sense of. It's larger than life. He'd always say that. He'd say that whenever I asked why he kept it braided instead of letting it down "to do whatever."

My mom won't let me cut it. It's larger than life.

To use an old phrase: a blast from my super-fricking embarrassing junior high past.

I laugh as I think about the surreality of it, and Kennedy, being the only one tuned in enough to hear me laughing at my phone like an idiot, asks, "What?"

With a glance up at her, I smile, wink, shake my head. It's the tangible creation of all the things I'm feeling inside.

I spent a large portion of seventh grade crushing on London Silva. I spent all of eighth grade becoming friends with London Silva.

That same year, miles and miles of maybe-more-than-but-not-quite friendship under our belts, London Silva was the first boy ever to kiss me.

@leirbagavlis is Gabriel Silva. "gls" is Gabriel London Silva. Gabriel L. Silva is London Silva.

The lifting, weightless thing I felt then, at the time of the kiss I knew was coming but didn't know how to want—I recall that now. I don't even know where to start with untangling this thing. The achy, blue knot of emotions sitting just below my collarbones. I'd call it off if I could. Strangely, it's the same colorful smudge of questioning I got when I realized that the very next night, he and his family had moved away without warning.

And London and I, we never talked again.

"Torr!" Auburn yells, and I almost drop my phone, hoping like hell I haven't accidentally favorited something from sixteen weeks ago.

I grab my phone up quick and confirm that I'm safe.

"We're trying to figure out food." Emery's eyes narrow at me. "What are you doing?"

"Nunya."

"Very mature, Torrey. Excellent and totally not suspicious at all."

Clarke yells, loud enough for the entire hall to hear—yes, even over the music and voices outside the room—"Oh, my God, are you cruising for porn?"

"Shut up, Smallville. I got your dad in my contacts if I need something qui—"

I absolutely, 100 percent deserve the fist she sends flying at my biceps. She laughs it off and then continues the conversation about where we could get some baller Mexican food on short notice, this time of night.

This is the college town area of the Bay, there's gotta be

gentrified Mexican food to be found here somewhere.

Back inside the relative safety of my DMs—*relative* being the operative word—I type a million things and then backspace them, then immediately panic that he's probably watching the TYPING . . . line appear and then disappear, appear and then disappear.

My thumbs fly, uncoordinated, across the screen's keys, and I hit send before I can think better (or worse) of it.

@returnoftheMcKenzie: Holy shit indeed. London, right? London Silva.

@leirbagavlis: just Gabriel now, haha. or Gabe. no one but my mom calls me London lol

Kennedy and Auburn stand and stretch. "We're gonna pee and then we'll go, yeah?" Auburn says. Clarke, Emery, and I, all prisoners of social media, grunt and/or nod in reply.

@returnoftheMcKenzie: You never did like that name

He really didn't. He let me call him that, but not because I was anyone special. It was because I was, like, maybe one of four people at school who wasn't using it to shove him around or calling him Brit Boy or, worse, Brit Girl. Because apparently "London" is GIRLS ONLY in the names department. Who knew.

@leirbagavlis: it grew on me

I glance at his tiny photo icon again. Lots of things grew on—

Another transparent TYPING . . . line from him floats up on the screen.

@leirbagavlis: how've you been? you look good in your photos, finally got some height huh? haha

I've been short all my life. That is, up until about last summer when I finally pushed over five-foot-ten and settled somewhere around five-eleven. I'd been just barely kissing five-six until maybe a year before. Hopefully there are a few more inches to go.

@returnoftheMcKenzie: Lol, thanks, I think. And yeah. Height finally found me.

Not unlike you, I think to myself.

@returnoftheMcKenzie: Looks like I'm not the only one who's changed

The words are coming easier now. It'd always been pretty easy to talk to London—Gabe. Gabriel.

@returnoftheMcKenzie: You're working with your hair now, looks like

I tap over and briefly scroll through his section of photos that other people have tagged him in. His hair is a bleeding blend of orange and gold watercolor. In most of these photos, it's a coil of curls running down past his shoulders, slung all the way over on one side.

He looks amazing. I hold my breath for four seconds and then hop back over to our messages.

@leirbagavlis: Yeah. I am. Had to. My mom still won't let me cut it.

This is my shocked face. I run a hand over my fade. I been wearing it like this for a few years now. Letting the top do whatever, managing it with a brush, a good barber, a skin taper, and a curl sponge.

@returnoftheMcKenzie: lol jesus. so where are you at now?

I hesitate with this next thing. But how can I not ask?

@returnoftheMcKenzie: your family left all quick. nobody even knew y'all was leaving.

TYPING . . .

@leirbagavlis: Yeah, I didn't know either. My dad got some immediate relocation thing from his job. Better healthcare and that.

@returnoftheMcKenzie: to where?

@leirbagavlis: Cincy.

@returnoftheMcKenzie: OHIO?

@leirbagavlis: You know any other places going short by cincy???

@returnoftheMcKenzie: lmao ok asshole, fine, don't get cute

@returnoftheMcKenzie: so ohio, jesus. what do people even DO in ohio?

@leirbagavlis: Meth

I laugh hysterically, and Emery glances up at me, all, *your weird is fucking with my ability to ignore you and while we're here is there something you'd like to tell me?*

"What the hell is that funny to you? I'm trying to figure out how we're gonna talk them out of making me eat thirteen-dollar burritos for the next four years, and you're laughing at cat videos on the Internet."

My phone buzzes in my hand.

@leirbagavlis: no seriously tho, I'm tripping out right now.

I looked for you online and shit but couldn't find you. I'm back in Cali now tho.

No one who actually lives in California calls it "Cali." No one. And if you are someone who does, turn your location on.

I just wanna talk.

@returnoftheMcKenzie: I just started using FB and Insta like, last year-ish

It hits me. Back in California. He's back. Here. Ish. Was that a lead? Is he throwing me a rope? If so, I probably just missed my chance to catch it.

@leirbagavlis: seriously? ALL late.

@returnoftheMcKenzie: Shut up. I'm here.

@leirbagavlis: yeah. you are.

Clarke rides on my back for the entire walk to the taco place, so I don't really have a chance to message Gabriel back until we get there, order, and are all tucking into our wet burritos, tacos, flautas, and enchiladas de mole.

@returnoftheMcKenzie: so you know we gotta talk about it, right?

Not like me. To do this. To initiate this particular topic of conversation. But here I am. I think I'm high on endorphins from carrying Clarke all the way here. That has to be it. Either that or I've been drugged. I glance around at the four girls sitting at our table.

Teletubbies. The whole bunch of them.

@leirbagavlis: talk about what

@returnoftheMcKenzie: come on, man

TYPING . . .

@leirbagavlis: haha alright I see you. Fine. Talk about it.

@returnoftheMcKenzie: eighth grade. you kissed me.

@leirbagavlis: I did

@returnoftheMcKenzie: And then you left

@leirbagavlis: I did. Not by choice tho. Plus that kiss was barely long enough to be anything.

It was long enough. Long enough to feel like healing.

@returnoftheMcKenzie: So you're what now? Gay? Bi? Straight/a queer-baiting asshole?

@leirbagavlis: I mean, I don't even know man. Bi is what I tell people.

@returnoftheMcKenzie: So you're out

@leirbagavlis: yeah, but I have a girlfriend. So. That kinda shit stops mattering when you're in love and shit.

@returnoftheMcKenzie: love, huh?

What does that even mean? I'm eighteen. I've been in what I thought was love once, but it died quietly, like a balloon losing helium over time. Our death took maybe a month. Right before prom, too. Jerk.

I hit the lock button on my phone immediately, shutting out the conversation like I can hide from it so long as it can't see me. Shit.

Shit, shit, shit. He has a girlfriend. Didn't see that coming.

Which is so dumb, because literally, in every movie I've ever seen where people reconnect there is always a preexisting relationship.

Name me one example in recent media where both parties reunite and are single and available. Just one. If you Google it right now, I'll know, so don't even think about it.

Anxious in the weirdest way, I tap into his profile again. I scroll through his posts, but there's nothing on his page that I can see. No cute-ass pictures of them, no tags for #wcw, no rhyming lines of iambic pentameter as captions.

It's taking me too long to respond now. He'll probably notice. I swipe backward, into our conversation again.

@returnoftheMcKenzie: nice

"Nice?" What in the hell kinda response . . .

@leirbagavlis: I mean, I don't know. It's new and we been friends for a minute. We're trying to figure it out. And since we're here, ngl, I wanted to go for longer

@returnoftheMcKenzie: longer?

@leirbagavlis: I wanted to kiss you. For longer than I did.

I lock the phone again. He's jumping around so much, I can't track where he's going with any of this. I shovel a forkful of Mexican rice into my mouth, the tiny bits of tomato and fresh onion on top becoming what should have been a satisfying combination. My taste buds have other plans.

With a glance over at Emery, I ask, "Dare me?"

"Dare you to what?" she says, mouth full of mole.

I set my fork down, lean sideways, close as I can get to her ear, and whisper, "I'm on the verge of sending a risky-as-hell DM. Dare me to do it." I need her to. If she doesn't, there's no way I'm ever going to be able to log into my Insta account ever again.

"I dare you."

"Yeah?"

"Yeah."

I hesitate.

"Do it," she commands. And then she snatches the phone out of my hand, and holy shit I think I'm going to throw up a whole bunch of lengua right now as I reach in her direction, where she is, right now, skimming my DMs with Gabriel, index finger moving too quickly. She stiff-arms me and continues to read. And before I can put her in a headlock or, I don't know, sneeze into her plate of food, she hands it back.

"Goddamn. Do it, Torr." She smirks.

Wet Willies are supposed to be juvenile and mildly disgusting but somehow I just haven't grown out of using them as a tactic for payback. Which Emery learns the hard way. And she shrieks so loud with laughter, and probably also some horror, that heads turn.

"What the hell is wrong with you two?" Auburn says.

"Nothing," we chorus together and then stare at each other.

I shake my head and send it before I can psych myself out.

@returnoftheMcKenzie: Except you punked out

Palms beginning to sweat, I need to forget how high this conversation is making me feel, so I jump over to my thread with Lisa and text, *Hey, any more info for me on this whole thing? I think we should probably sit down with someone on this, maybe?*

Phone locked, I then shovel six tacos con lengua into my gut as fast as God and also Jesus will allow.

And after Auburn tells five very unfunny penis jokes and Clarke almost chokes on a mouthful of asada fries, we make the walk back to campus, where students are still milling, though things are much quieter than they were earlier.

I don't like it. You know why? I'll tell you why. It's because once I'm back in my room lying on my bare-ass saltine cracker of a mattress, I start to think. Too much time to think just brings me back home. Too much time to think—especially when Desh is MI-freaking-A—allows too many of the whispers to seep in.

How in the hell is it possible that I made it out just a moment before the universe would require me to tuck back in? There's a moment where I just spend, like, ten minutes imagining I don't go back home or admit that I abandoned my bees or that I lied to Uncle Miles when I told him I'd always find him there, in the apiary.

That promise? That was just moments before he died in the shittiest hospital in east LA. It's not the kind of thing you renege on.

Around 3:30 a.m., I wake up with the remnants of a nascent dream on my lips as Desh kaleidoscopes his way back into the room and onto his mattress. He's asleep within seconds, not a single sound made aside from the heavy inhale-exhale action he's got going.

I turn over onto my stomach, taking in as large a breath as possible, soaking in all the honey-scented memories that talk Baldwin Hills into being some kind of sweetness.

Sweetness.

Sweet things.

I open my Instagram back up, and sure enough, there's that paper airplane up there telling me I have a new message. Somehow, opening it at nearly 4:00 a.m. is easier. Feels like it's just me and whatever's written in the message.

Stupid, I know. Don't judge me.

@leirbagavlis: Hey, here's my number. Do you maybe want to like, text instead?

And his big, dumb, stupid ten-digit phone number is sitting right there.

And I don't even waste the space of a moment keying the number sequence I may already have memorized into my phone.

ME: Hey, it's Torr

ME: *Torrey. This is Torrey, I mean.

ME: Torrey McKenzie

Wow. I'm extra as hell right now.

GABRIEL: I know who you are, Torr

Super extra, but also very okay with him calling me Torr. I'm into it—to the surprise of absolutely no one.

ME: *What are you doing up?*

GABRIEL: *What are YOU doing up*

ME: *Touché. My roommate just came in. Couldn't sleep after that.*

GABRIEL: *How is your roomie? Cool?*

ME: *I know him a little bit. He's cool. SFSU does this thing where they connect you with your dorm- and suitemates ahead of time.*

GABRIEL: *Wait what? You're at SFSU?*

Did I stutter?

GABRIEL: *I promise I'm not stalking you on some weird shit, but I am at SFSU.*

GABRIEL: *Also. As a student. Attending this school.*

Did he stutter?

ME: *So this means . . . you are on campus? Right now? Wait, are you dorming?*

This is a commuter college, but the dorm population is still pretty substantial. I have to slow my fingers down with intent as they fly across my screen. My phone is starting to get warm from all the use it's getting.

Lock the phone. Hold the phone as tight as possible to your chest. Realize you are ten seconds away from scribbling Mr. Torrey Silva *into your notebook. Plug your phone in to charge, you idiot. Do not open it again—*

Okay, fine. After that time, do not open it again to check for a response that hasn't come after four minutes. Five minutes. Eighteen . . . twenty minutes.

Do not keep checking for a reply that probably isn't coming.
Pat yourself on the back. You've ruined it before things have even
gotten started. Like sneezing on someone else's birthday cake just
before the off-key "Happy Birthday" chorus could even shoot off.

I stick my phone under my pillow and close my eyes. Something hot and heavy hits me about the fact that I am not in my bed at home, where Theo sleeps downstairs in his drafty basement and Aunt Lisa snores indelicately just across the hall.

This is new, and suddenly my skin is on fire.

I'm not saying I'm about to start hyperventilating. But do you happen to have a paper bag I can breathe into right now?

Okay. Focus. Breathe. Think.

I can do this.

My hand snakes back under my pillow to once again retrieve my still-hot, overworked phone.

I'm on the university's website faster than Apple can drop its next iPhone upgrade. Add/Drop.

The crucial deadline after class registration where you can add or drop courses without penalty to your GPA or your pockets.

That's two weeks from now. Two weeks.

That's a pretty solid amount of time. Fourteen days. That's 336 hours.

Don't worry. That's not an offhand fact I just so happen to know. Google is powerful.

Two weeks is enough time to settle things both here and back home. Because I like this place. And I think I kind of need it.

I need these people and these opportunities and—

I won't verbalize that last one. But, basically, Gabriel. I . . . yeah.

Remotely, I could take these two weeks while my options to add/drop are open and try to fix this mess with my apiary from here. I've got that much time to alter my class schedule before I can be penalized financially for it anyway, so I've got an okay amount of wiggle room to figure this mess out.

Mess. Messes. Speaking of messy . . . I gotta call Theo.

I let my phone drop from my hand and stare up at the ceiling for a moment before the stillness has a chance to take hold. I pull my shirt off just before the flames of newness, loss, and rejection can swallow me.

'm not sure which is preferable: A wake up from my university-issued alarm clock—a hair-raising alarm bell meant only to startle—or the person on the other end of my phone line, ringing me at 7:00 a.m.

It's a number I know too well. The San Francisco area code gives it away, but I have to squint at the phone for a minute to get my dry eyes to focus. It's what I get for falling asleep with my contacts in again.

"Hello?"

"Hello, Torrey. This is Loretta calling from God Willing Hospice Care."

"Yeah, hi, Loretta. I know where you're calling from."

"Good. We're calling to see if maybe this month you'd like to take care of your mother's billing on time or if you'll be calling at the last minute to request another payment arrangement."

See. She just out here being hateful. Loretta has called us every month for two years. Before I was of age, she was calling Theo and Uncle Miles. But every minute of those two years she was on us, Loretta has hated my stupid guts.

And another shit thing is, what the hell is up with that name? "God Willing"?

What?

God willing, your loved one will live to see another day and also maybe if they've abused too many pharmaceutical drugs, they won't actually have to live out their days as a vegetable at some shitty-but-still-too-expensive inpatient care center in the Bay.

I'm sorry, you want people checking their family members in to feel like life is *maybe* possible? Like, well, I mean, you could stay here but, you know, if God says you gotsta go, *you gotsta go.*

How much would you bet me God won't get up off His ass to do jack shit for my mom?

She did it to herself anyway.

"Have you talked to Theo?" I ask. Theo is always the first option for paying my mom's monthly. If he decides he's too crotchety to take care of it, they default to me. I know that if they're calling me now, Theo's already told them to wipe their own asses with it.

Here's another gamble: How much would you be willing to bet those were his exact words?

I always thought living closer would ensure I stayed on top of this stuff; it's a large part of the reason I picked the schools I applied to. I just needed to be closer to her.

To handle her healthcare. Just to handle the healthcare stuff.

"Mr. McKenzie has already requested we not bother him with it."

I'm not going to ask Loretta to elaborate on the wording he used, but I feel like this probably means I won our bet. I got Venmo, Cash App, Ko-fi, and PayPal.

"Okay, uh. I'm going to have to call you back. Like, later. At a later date. To set something up."

The key is to be vague here. Smooth. But I'm locked out apparently, and so all that just seems as obvious as watching a twelve-foot woman tap dance down the street.

New-student orientation is, for the most part, mandatory. About half the planned events are required. Which is why, after sleeping through the Breakfast Mixer (yes, everything is a Mixer, don't ask me why, ask the white people who plan these things), Desh and

I drag our sorry asses down to the quad, a massive grassy hill, to hear the president of SFSU (she tells us to just call her "Carol") talk about . . . SFSU.

We really only attend this "mandatory" thing for the free food, but it's just our luck that we were idiots, didn't check the time, and arrive just as all the food is being finished.

I pull my Ray-Bans down onto my face. Definitely could have just read up on this school, you know, on the Internet. Like, before I applied to it.

But okay, go off, I guess.

I take a long drag off the very large black coffee in my hand, the heat of it doing things to my body that I am regretting in the moment but will appreciate in approximately ninety minutes. Desh does the same to his iced something or other, licking caramel and whipped cream out of its dome top.

My phone buzzes in my pocket, and I snatch it out so fast, I almost catapult my hot coffee right at Just-Call-Me-Carol.

Turns out it's just Emery texting to find out where in the crowd we are.

So, if you couldn't tell, I still have not received a text back from him.

I don't even care though. No BFD.

Shut up.

There are bigger, more important things to worry about. My farm, for example. As soon as this mandatory shit is over, I'm hopping on the phone to make some calls. There's supposed to be some kind of Meet-Your-RA thing happening after this, but I'm only willing to take things so far with this school right now. The apiary's a priority. Uncle Miles is a priority.

"God, finally, I find you guys. This crowd is dumb huge," Emery says. Her thick, dark hair is in two buns, one on each side of her head. I flick one, and she smacks my hand.

"Do not fuck up my space buns, Torrey, I will actually castrate you."

Desh laughs, sips his coffee. Ass.

The crowd is suddenly clapping and I look around, my own golf clap in full effect.

"Why are we clapping?" Desh asks.

Glad I'm not the only one.

"I don't know," Emery adds. Excellent, we are zero for three. "When can we leave? I need to pee."

This girl. Em's bladder is in charge of her life and not the other way around. But that doesn't stop us from taking our sweet time, wandering around campus—a thing that is supposed to be handled via a mandatory campus tour sometime tomorrow. We find a bathroom after stopping at two different ones first, none of which are to Em's liking.

Seriously, what is the process for girls when they pee? Why y'all do it in pairs? Why y'all take so long? How many times are you going to remind us that y'all have a couch in there and we don't?

And while she's in there, Desh is talking about how there's a Guided Meditation Mixer and then a Fun-and-Games Mixer. Meanwhile, I'm over here chewing my nails to the quick as girls and their stupidly good-smelling perfumes waft past us as they dance in and out of the bathroom.

We are probably standing way too close.

And I think some of the ladies are disgusted by the way I'm basically cannibalizing on my own hand. It's the need to be back there at home. Handling business. It's ridiculous that it's already past noon, and I haven't even heard from Lisa with any news or updates yet.

So I text. Because I'm impatient, I haven't learned not to jump the gun on things. Yet. And also because—here's some transparency—if I can put off speaking to Theo, I'm going to go out of my way to do it. Speaking to Theo about literally anything is going to be filed in the encyclopedia under the Hot Pile of Garbage entry. But speaking to Theo about this? About the bees, the apiary—Theo's favorite subject, things that matter to me . . . those instances are never not steeped in some low-level kind of trauma.

ME: Hey, you talk to Theo? I send to Lisa. Is this considered delegating or punking out? Don't answer. It's just an observation.

Aunt Lisa doesn't text back right away. But when she does, it's not pretty.

LISA: The fact that you're away at college and could be doing it up out there and forgetting everything and everyone up in this

place and yet HERE YOU ARE in my texts, about the farm.
Patience, Torrey.

Those three little gray dots pop up. I feel like Apple should just remove that feature from iMessage altogether, because honestly, it's not doing anything good for nobody's blood pressure.

She doesn't send anything else though. And I'm surprised, because Black girls and their ability to completely obliterate you via text messages is legend.

A cluster of chills riots its way down my back. If Lisa walks, the farm will keep running. There are people who help out occasionally, people from the neighborhood who know business, who knew Uncle Miles, and who helped me when I was running things there. But the thing is, those people aren't Lis. I can't trust them the way I can trust her.

Sure, Mrs. Jericho is nice. She's baked us gluten-free banana bread every year for Christmas for as long as I've lived with Theo. She's not young anymore, though. She helps out of the goodness of her heart, but she and everyone else understands that her good heart could give out any day now.

Then there are the twins, Mr. Finn and Mr. Turner (I'm really not sure on the validity of twinship or even blood relation at all, but they look an awful lot alike and so everybody just runs with it), brothers who never married and never left the city and now that they're pushing sixty-plus, I'm not sure they have any intentions to change that. They take care of the farm's upkeep and garden structure.

Not gonna lie, a lot of the easiness of running the apiary was handed down to me along with its title.

Still, I'm worried that if Lisa isn't there to keep her eye and heart on the grounds, things will fall apart. Faster than they already are. I feel a hot iron sort-of throb in the back of my eye, and it's bleeding quickly into my jaw.

A migraine. Remember those little shits from earlier? Yep. It's the beginnings of a good one that, if I don't head it off now, will take me out hard.

My phone's in my back pocket for only a half second before it vibrates again.

"Okay, ready?" Emery says, exiting the bathroom.

Phone in hand, I mumble something noncommittal as I glance down to see that, yep, he texted back.

GABRIEL: *Hey, sorry. Got caught up trying to update family and stuff about move-in. So. Yeah. To answer your question. I'm dorming. I'm over at Cervantes Hall for now, till they reassign me to the arts dorm.*

Arts?

GABRIEL: *Where you at? Wanna grab a coffee or something?*

No. No, I really don't. At the moment I kind of just want for someone to cut into me. I want to disappear. Which, I guess, is why I walk away from Desharu and Emery without a word and dial up my granddad.

Excedrin Migraine, here I come.

*P*ause right here.

Theopolis James McKenzie spends his days in a back-yard among plants and things as dead as he is, arguing with anyone who will let him about his need to return back home to the deepest of the deep south—Louisiana's simultaneously quiet and loud streets, still just carefully arranged rubble after Katrina.

He forgets that it was an argument that brought him and his young wife—my late grams, Belinda—here. A personal belief that he deserved to live in "an affluent neighborhood." Like, him, specifically. He deserved that. Not poor Black people from the bayou's hood, in general.

And I understand why. I can tell the dust of his honey-soft drawl is his last reminder of what "home" actually is. He's worked hard to deny it all this time. He's lied to himself for so long that he's maybe even started to believe it. That he could come here to this beachy, coastal sandpit and not look back at the things that made him great.

It's become my job to remind him that an airplane ride will likely kill him. He's too old for anything that doesn't promise him his own wings and a good burial. So he stays. He stays on the Hill, and he rages and he sits in that goddamn rusting fold-out chair in the backyard with his breakneck posture, spitting at the idea that his only son is gone.

And, selfishly, since Uncle Miles died, I've learned I'm not quite ready to be alone.

So I do the same. Did the same. I stayed with Theo. With his just-shy-of-cruel demeanor and his judgment about who I am and who I love.

Uncle Miles used to always make me promise I'd take care of the family. But he's ruining that, Theo is. And if I lose the apiary because of him, I'll make Theo sorry he ever brought my family here in the first place.

It'd be nice to deny that Theo is my last resort for everything. But the truth is, I don't even list him as my emergency contact for school because typically you don't want an emergency contact who would answer the phone during an emergency with a delayed, "What are you on my phone for now?"

He's an "in case of death" contact. Emergencies don't warrant enough of a fuck to give.

So, me . . . this? Calling him now? That's dumb. But Uncle Miles is the reason I did any of this at all. The reason I took over the care and handling of the apiary. The reason I did just enough to get away from the city but not leave the state entirely because of a promise to care, on any level, for his father.

Uncle Miles is worth this. He's said the same damn thing about me time and time again.

You're worth it, b. You're worth the world, kid.

That mattered.

Alright. You can hit play.

"This is Theo," he answers at his own pace.

I know he's not busy, but I ask anyway. "I catch you at a bad time?"

Wish I could say it's a wonder he didn't feel the need to give me the heads-up that all the work I've done for four years—since freshman year—is going being swallowed by the city's need to gentrify every viable part of the hood that young Black kids use to stay out of trouble. The community center was first. Then the local playground. Mr. Johnson's parking-lot garden was uprooted—no pun intended—and is now, to my knowledge, going to serve as a small, insignificant piece of the new mall's three-story parking garage.

"Thought I told you not to call me 'less you was dyin'."

"It's important. About the letter?"

He's silent. But not because he's unaware. He just always feels the need to make me work for shit. Maybe it's the only entertainment he ever gets.

"Off top, Theo. I'm talking about the apiary right now," I continue. Really, this is no way to speak to your grandfather, but the man makes me call him by his first name and that's not even the weirdest part of this relationship.

It's always been that way between him and me. His name is on the space Uncle Miles built his dream on. I worked two and a half jobs—one of which was the apiary—and kept my head down while I tried to graduate from high school without a drug habit or an arrest record. And as far as I was aware, Theo was keeping everything legitimate on his end, too.

"You read the thing?" he asks. As though I'd have called him without doing exactly that.

"Yes, Theo, I read the letter."

I hear him lean back in that same rickety old foldout chair he's always in. That same chair that's practically become a part of the backyard he planted it in a decade ago.

"What's it say, Torrey?"

I roll my eyes. If I weren't all but trapped inside the walls of this school, he might've reached through the phone and snatched my ass.

Because I know—I know—he can tell I just disrespected him that way.

And do you know what? So much of that shit just becomes

irrelevant when your skin starts to feel like it's holding in raging storms, and earthquakes start to erupt just behind your eyelids.

"It says the farm's property is being seized, Theo," I say, begging now. "Jesus Christ, please tell me this didn't all happen without me knowing about it?"

He would have had to get first notices, second notices, appeals information—if he even bothered to go that route and file the paperwork properly—all before this appeal denial that basically meant my soul was getting put up for some white people's "I'm an ally of the gangsters, too!" sale.

None of which Theo was inclined to care about. The only person it would really mean something to . . . is me. And I guess, just like every other person who decides I don't deserve to matter, the root of my soul isn't worth him putting in the work for.

"Boy, quit playing on this phone. What's done is done."

I'm squeezing the phone so tight, my knuckles feel as though they're splitting, the skin peeling away from itself the way my lips want to part on a scream.

"You fix this. You need to fix this, Theo—"

"I'm old and I'm tired and don't you dare raise your voice at me like you ain't got no sense, boy. I'm 'bout ready to be done with this farm and these bees and your ass, too. Been in this too long watching your Nancy ass dance around this hell-city talking about honey. My boy is gone, and now that Echo Park dirt trap will be, too." He's breathing hard. That whole outburst took a lot out of him, and I'm just sick enough to be happy about the fact that he is physically suffering here.

But, still, he's not finished. "You want information? Here's all you gon' get. I did fix it. I fixed it so that someone else can come in and take over and get that farm out this neighborhood. I fixed it so that I won't have to die before that farm does. I fixed it so that they'll come and essentially lock you out of that mess within the next thirty days. I don't give a gray rat's ass *what* happens with that farm, which is exactly why it's all set to be auctioned off. *There* is your fix."

And he's off the phone before I can really understand the way my chest has fractured irreparably. Thirty days and they're going to claim the land and close it off? Thirty days? Auction?

It's going to be sold off to the highest goddamned bidder? It feels like that abrupt end to the call has completely obliterated my ability to breathe. Maybe all the damage that's been done here will end me. I have to. I have to do it. Thirty days to fix things, and everyone is working against me.

8.

*T*he cool thing about living with Desh is that, although he's a cyclone of a human when it comes to cleanliness, I've noticed that at night, when it's just the two of us hanging in there, not quite feeling the whole six-to-eight-hours-of-sleep thing, he's a really nice presence to have around.

My head's been in turmoil basically since the second I got here. And I suspect that Desh has calculated this plan to keep me as occupied as possible during the day and then letting me process and internalize at night. I'm glad he's in that bed across from mine, the blue light of his entirely-too-close-to-his-face phone the only other light in the room aside from my own.

I pull my phone out, knowing I should have returned Gabriel's text long before now.

ME: *For sure. Coffee could be cool. Wanna go on campus or off?*

Coffee could be cool? What is wrong with me?

Please don't answer that.

I text Lisa again because I need somebody. You know that feeling, right? Where you just need somebody, anybody really, to care about you down to your marrow. Someone who'll make you their number one. That's Lisa for me. It was Uncle Miles, but I think Lis got passed the buck when he died. Guess she inherited me just like Theo did. Only difference is, Lisa isn't a two-faced son of a bitch.

ME: *Love you, Lis.*

LISA: *I love you, too, buggy. You alright? Settled in okay? Need anything? I can look up directions to see if there's a Target or something nearby so you can get whatever you need, maybe I can gift it to you online somehow. I miss you already.*

ME: *I'm good, Lis. Thank you tho. I miss you, too.*

ME: *I'm sorry. I love you. Please don't be mad at me. You love me, I know you do.*

LISA: *I do. Which is why I can say this: Don't come home to deal with the farm. Please don't ruin what you've got there. This is big. The first generation in the family to even go to college? Yeah. Keep that for yourself. Don't let this neighborhood take that from you.*

She's right. It's not a fact I've forgotten. Just one that I occasionally need to be reminded has some pretty heavy significance.

Slauson Avenue will take everything from you if you let it.

ME: Okay. I promise. I'll stick it out.

And no sooner do I get that out to her, an email dings on my phone.

The subject line and email preview tell me it's one of my professors emailing about the textbooks and reading required for class on the first day. I've been a college student for two whole-ass days and already I have homework? Dormwork? Educational BS that I have to prioritize?

Lisa has this thing about priorities. Hers are usually pretty sordid. Like, she's all about her hair appointments over paying whatever bills she's got sitting on her neck.

But that's Black women. Hair and nails and skin over everything.

It's nice that she's helped me see the value in creating my own. But right now, I gotta say this is the first time I've ever really felt like I don't know which items on my priorities list go in what order.

Although, after having just promised Lisa that I'd keep my head down and keep it pushing, I need to commit to at least getting through the first week or so. Admissions has been packed since I got here, anyway. So the only way I'm talking to them (sans a two-hour wait time) about disenrollment is when classes officially begin and things have evened out.

So I resolve to wait a week before I try to talk to anybody about withdrawing or postponing or whatever the hell my options are.

I click into the email and find a link for the ENG 101 course I'm in for. I barely passed that part of the entry exam. My scores were on their last gasping breath, *just* high enough to get me above the you-need-to-take-the-basic-ass-prerequisites point.

I need five whole-ass textbooks for this class. Five of them. And the least expensive of them is $48.

Christ. My financial aid barely covers tuition, dorm fees, move-in expenses, and my meal card. I'm back at square one. I have $100 in my pocket, and that was just what Lisa gave me as a graduation present.

The email does contain a number of short essays and literary pieces that I would otherwise have to purchase separately, and I still can't afford that shit. Lisa, of course, has been financing everything over here. And won't accept any "I'll handle it" Black man machismo bullshit.

Still, a new bucket of stress is poured down the back of my neck. It is slimy and it is cold and it is also ridiculously heavy.

GABRIEL: Might as well stick with on campus since we really should know where that shit is at, no?

The little notification slides its way down the top of my phone then gets sucked back up, and I swap over into it from my email app.

Next to me, Desh is falling asleep in five-minute bursts, then waking up to resume the watching of a thread of Vines that's been posted on Twitter.

I only know because he keeps quote retweeting them and

tagging me in them. There's been, like, fourteen so far.

ME: Haha, yeah for sure.

GABRIEL: I mean, lissen. If you don't want to, it's cool you know.

Shit. My mood is bleeding into this conversation. I'm just still in a haze about the cost of these textbooks for only one of my five classes this semester.

And all the reading I gotta do beforehand? That's almost fifty pages.

ME: No, I do. Sorry. I'm barely away rn.

Lie. I am not going to find sleep anytime soon.

ME: *awake

Gotta make it believable.

ME: I'm just stressing it about the price of these textbooks only white people can afford.

GABRIEL: Right? I got an email this morning that was basically like: READ 80 PAGES WITHIN THE HOUR AND ALSO BUY 80 TEXTBOOKS ALL PRICED AT $80 EACH.

ME: Oh, that's verbatim or?

GABRIEL: I mean, yeah, pretty much that is kind of exactly what the email said mostly.

ME: I see.

A little of the trash that's been forcefully kissing its way down my neck is lessened by a fraction. A very noticeable, extremely Gabe-tinged fraction.

ME: I'm surprised you're up

GABRIEL: *Are you.*

Not a question. Just, oh, are you. Wondering. About me during this filth hour of the night? I love it when boys do this.

I whisper, "Torrey, what?"

"Huh?" Desh says, startling awake. But he's asleep again before I can even get some kind of lie going.

ME: It's not exactly standard business hours. What's got you burning the midnight oil?

Burning the midnight—what the hell is wrong with me?

Like, listen. I'm not new at this. People have this tendency to joke about being eighteen and in love and shit. But I know my way around some flirty banter. I was twelve when I had my first boyfriend. Whatever that means at twelve. We held hands under the table at lunch. We were partners for group projects. We saved each other seats during assemblies. That kinda thing. His name was Tristan Quirk and we "dated" for like, I don't know, however long it took for us to graduate sixth grade and head off to different middle schools.

Anyway, neither Tristan nor I was out at that age. One of Theo's favorite pastimes was—and remains to this day—making gay jokes, using the word as an insult, and calling men who use body wash over bar soap the kind of slurs that run red across a gay kid's vision.

The same went for Uncle Miles and all his older friends that I, beyond all reason, wanted to be cool enough to kick it with. It's probably a thing that should've made it really hard for me to love and worship my uncle the way I did. The way I still do.

But the thing is, that's just what it means to grow up gay in the Black community. It's like homophobia is the cishet Black community's lifeblood.

Anyway, I digress.

My point: With one look, I got Tristan Quirk to walk home using a different route than our friends. One "what's up?" lift of my chin. A different route—my route—delivered on whatever finesses was inherent in my twelve-year-old body's crooked smile.

So, burning the midnight oil . . . that's new. A trip. Confusing. And not a super great look.

But then, I guess, maybe it wasn't such a bomb? Because, Jesus Herman Christ, he sends me a picture, and I am not ready.

He is on his bed—fully clothed, don't worry, your pearls may remain unclutched—smiling as some kid behind him, another Black guy, tries to hang a Deadpool banner up behind him.

GABRIEL: My temp roommate is a comic book fan. I almost want to ask Admissions to let me stay in this dorm. Business majors are hilarious.

ME: You're into comics?

GABRIEL: No, I am actually not!

GABRIEL: But even if I was, I'd still be infinitely cooler than you and your "burning the midnight oil" lookin ass

I die.

I throw my phone, and it lands on our shitty carpet-over-cement floor, and I die and die and die.

And then Desh wakes up, unlocks his phone, and tags me in another Vine.

@DESHperateHousewives: @ReturnoftheMcKenzie yo, I'm weak rn

But he's actually not. He's practically comatose. And this time I think he's probably gonna stay that way because he slides down his pillow, half his body basically hanging off the bed, and drops his phone, too.

And he still doesn't wake up.

I do something dumb. Which is standard operating procedure.

I lean over, a snoring, mouth-all-kinds-of-open-like-your-loud-Aunt-Ruth's-mouth-at-the-cookout Desh just behind and to the left of me. Phone back in hand, I snap a quick photo (okay, fine, it's more like eight or nine photos) of him and me and send it to Gabriel with the cry-laugh emoji.

ME: Blame his snoring, it's screwing with my ability to use relevant slang!

There's a long delay in his response and if I have to wait however many days or hours for him to reply again, I'm going to lose it and throw a baby llama into the ocean or something.

But he texts back like ten minutes later, just as I'm about to doze off.

GABRIEL: You really can't send me pics like that.

Shit.

Shoot.

Shit. Did I mess up? Do I tell him I was only joking, or would that be super childish? Desh won't care if I took any number of photos of him. Awake, sleeping, naked, dead. I'm willing to put money on the fact that giving a shit isn't his style. But maybe Gabriel's a stickler on stuff like that? Like, taking photos of people without their express permission and sending them to third parties.

ME: Oh haha. My bad. Desh is my boy tho, he'll think the pic is hilarious.

GABRIEL: No

GABRIEL: I just mean pictures

GABRIEL: Of you

GABRIEL: At night

GABRIEL: With no shirt on

Oh.

I swallow my heartbeat.

I don't text back. I honestly can't. Because how do you even respond to that with anything other than "God, you make my heart smile."

*O*rientation weekend comes and goes, and classes officially
start the following Tuesday.

Desh and CAKE spend the day bumming around Frisco
(which, I've learned, nobody who is actually from San Francisco
calls it "Frisco"), doing all the touristy bits like biking the Golden
Gate Bridge and hitting up Ghirardelli Square.

I know this, not because I make the wise and incredibly social
college-student decision to go with them, but because I spend
half that day checking their tweets and Instagram stories, and
the other half researching what I can do to appeal this decision
to snatch my farm.

The facts are these:

1. Yes, Lisa did in fact make me marathon *Pushing Daisies* post cancellation. Which, yo, is a sadness. And so dumb of—whatever network *Pushing Daisies* was even on, God, I can't even remember, can you? ABC?

2. The "notices" Theo would have gotten about the apiary had come on the heels of the state reaching out to him about the property taxes he never paid.

3. Theo was delinquent on two years' worth of unpaid property taxes. Which doesn't seem like much for a passion project turned bee farm in the Los Angeles ghettoes. But, again, gentrification, that sly bastard, had been increasing the property's value for the better half of a decade. Uncle Miles had swooped in and gotten things started just in time to turn a solid-enough profit each quarter.

4. There is a Facebook message board or group for literally anything these days, including, to my great pleasure, one where people in the thick of foreclosures can ask questions and/or vent their frustrations. I don't vent, but I do ask a couple of questions about what my options are, leaving my contact information in case anyone has any information that can help me. (That was some dumbass kid shit. So definitely keep this part in mind; it's gonna bite me in the ass later.)

5. I spend all day reading and learning whatever I can for

an approximate four minutes and twelve seconds of phone time with the State Personnel Board. Which is to say, I am actually on the phone for three hours. Two hours, fifty-five minutes, and forty-five seconds of that consists of me being on hold, listening to Whitney's "How Will I Know." Previously an incredible, timeless song. But now I have time on that bitch. I have two hours, fifty-five minutes, forty-five seconds and a beautifully detailed explanation of how, exactly, *you will know* that he loves your dumb ass.

6. I'm sorry, Whitney, RIP. I ain't mean it.

7. My next course of action is, I think, going to have to be filing an extension on the allotted time we're being given to vacate the premises. They give us a two-month lead time. That's bull.

8. Emery, my favorite little cupcake (don't tell Auburn), once mentioned in SFSU's online forum that she's been involved with this civil rights group (note to self: remember the name of said group before speaking to Em about it) who might have some resources, know-how, or pull with the city.

9. So, natch, I stay up until 4:44 (shout out HOV!) a.m. trying to figure out how to put that in motion.

Now, fast-forward to my dumb ass waking up at 8:16 a.m. the next morning, which is sixteen minutes past the start of my first-ever official college class.

I barely manage to pull my shirt on and grab my dorm key card before I book it out the door, a still sleeping, did-not-schedule-an-8:00-a.m.-class Desh snoring in a cloud of my dust.

Ever notice how there's always this, like, weird rule in life, where if you think you are at rock bottom, you know you had better keep that shit to yourself. Because nine times out of ten, the universe might just show up at your cocksucking house, all A BITCH HAD TIME TODAY! and kick you down rock bottom's stairs for shits and giggles.

So that's me, swearing to Jesus and Madonna and Cher and all them other one-name assholes that if I could just make it to this class and not have lost my spot, then I'd prioritize school and keep bees (haha, *keep bees*) on the back burner.

And I'm feeling pretty good about it for the first, eh, nine or so minutes I spend sprinting from the dorms. But then, oh sweet universe, I get lost.

And after I ask for directions and head in the exact opposite direction I just came from, I get lost again before finally finding the building, floor, and room number I'm supposed to be in for CIV 207: Advanced Civilizations II.

Which would be wonderful!

Except the doors are locked. And the only greeting I get is from a sign on the wall to the left of the double doors that reads, "LATE ON THE FIRST DAY? NOT COOL. SEE ME AFTER CLASS, AND I'LL LET YOU KNOW IF YOUR EXCUSE IS GOOD ENOUGH TO KEEP YOUR SPOT. I WOULDN'T

HOLD MY BREATH. —Dr. Lily Anderson"

I spend whatever's left of the hourlong class sitting on the floor directly across from that ugly sign. I swear that sign is laughing at me.

Up yours, sign. You're written in Comic Sans, nobody likes you anyway.

An exhale leaves me slumped farther down the wall.

How is it possible that I've messed up so royally already? Maybe this is just my life now. Maybe what I just do now is mess things up. Maybe Theo is right, and I've been chasing after some "romantic shit" with the apiary this entire time. He thinks I romanticize Uncle Miles's death by trying to keep his legacy alive in the bees.

Maybe Theo is right. And it's the worst thing, like ants crawling under the skin.

I hate failing. Don't you? I mean, who doesn't, y'know? But you want to know what I hate even more than failing?

Failing while Theo is watching. Failing and proving Theo right. Failing and confirming every stupid thing Theo has ever said about me. That I am a burden. That my sexuality and I have humiliated him. That everything I do, every way I feel and every part of who I am is inappropriate.

"I'm going to bet my lunch money that you're Torrey McKenzie."

The woman standing in front of me is very tall. Easily six feet or so. I glance up at her, dressed in a myriad of loose fabrics, half of which are sheer, all of which are dark in color. Gray or black or a mix.

Her hair is a shade I would definitely name Unnatural Orange. I'm mentioning the hair first so you can get a picture going. Curls. Super tight ones. And there are so many of them shits, it's ridiculous. This woman is Medusa in the flesh. And you bet your sweet ass I'm afraid of her.

She sucks her teeth. "Up, kid. Rule number one in my class is don't be late. Rule number two is don't ever keep a Latina waiting."

I wait for that stupid third rule, but it doesn't come because she turns on her Birkenstocked feet and walks back into the room.

Do I follow?

Duh! Of course I follow, weren't you just there, listening to what she said? Don't. Keep. A. Latina. Waiting. Bitch.

I add the bitch part because it felt implied. Like, she definitely wanted to call me a bitch, and you know what, I was gonna let her.

"You can call me Coco. Take a seat, McKenzie."

I take the seat immediately to my left because, honestly, I don't know what would happen if I took my time making it to the front of the decked-out auditorium-style classroom just to park my Black ass right in front of her.

Buuuuuuuut . . . then she comes at me with a single raised brow, and I have no choice but to get up and basically sprint to the front of the class.

How does she do this? Like, I've only met one college professor in my life so far, and if they're all this intimidating, I'm going to have to rethink my interest in higher education.

In front of her now (and seated, yes), I don't dare speak.

"You want this class, Torrey?"

"Yes, ma'am."

"You want to remain a student at this university and in this class in your 'Hello, I'm Green' clothing?"

Damn, like that? I didn't think I looked that young. How does someone wear the same shit they've been wearing for two years and still show up to college on a wave of lame-ass First-Time Freshman vibes?

"Yes, ma'am."

"Good. Grab a syllabus off the table on your way out the door. Before you come to my class each week, you're going to visit me in my office an hour prior, until further notice."

[extremely Lin-Manuel Miranda–as–Hamilton voice] I'm sorry, what?

"That's, like, 7:00 a.m. I'd have to be up—"

"On time. Yes." She nods. Steeples her fingers. I love her and I fear her and I hate her and I'm low-key trying to be her.

"Yes, ma'am?"

"Good. Haul ass out of here before my next class shows up."

I don't hesitate, except then she's shouting, "¡Ya! ¡La pinche sílaba!" and it doesn't take a genius to interpret her Spanish and realize I never grabbed a syllabus.

I double back. Grab it.

Do not make eye contact. And then I book it out of there.

College is stupid and emotionally exhausting but also kind of a thrill.

I 'm on my skateboard, doing damage to my trucks and bearings, the street half jackhammered apart as a result of too many years with no county aid, and I'm heading toward the apiary.

I kick my regular leg out and slow my speed down to greet Mrs. Jericho, who everyday, regardless of the weather, is outside watering her garden at exactly this time. Her very dead garden that probably won't ever make a comeback. But still, she's out there, back bowed by an unseen struggle and humming some soulful rendition of what is either "Wade In the Water" or Jon B's "They Don't Know."

"Hi, Mrs. Jericho," I call as my wheels click by.

She glances up slow, like molasses. "Oh, Torrey, hi, baby. How you doin'?"

"I'm okay, how are you?"

She rubs a spot low on her back as she stands upright. "Oh, don't you be out here worrying about me. You need to be better than just 'okay.' How we gon' get you a good woman otherwise?"

Yikes. Never fails. "Alright, Mrs. Jericho." I'm almost out of earshot now, but Mrs. Jericho didn't survive in this neighborhood for forty years by being quiet.

"My granddaughter would be perfect for you. She's a lawyer," she calls as I'm almost at the end of the block.

"I'm only eighteen, Mrs. Jericho."

"I'mma have her call your auntie," she shouts. "You be safe on that board!"

"I will, Mrs. Jericho." I take the left a little too hard and know internally that my body is falling toward an injury that will be catastrophic, my bones twisting in on themselves in some futile effort to save something. My balls shrivel up into my stomach and somehow I'm naked now because I land facedown and break my face in front of Coco's entire class.

I come awake in what I know is the most horrific fashion. The lights in the dorm are all off, save for Desh's reading light, a lighthouse across the way.

I'm trying to make this metaphor work for you, but I almost just used the sweat that's covering my body as some painted image of the ocean. So. I'll stop there.

You're welcome.

"You okay, Torr?" Desh is trying so hard not to laugh. I feel like I should commend him for this tremendous effort.

Before I answer Desh and tell him I'm kind of not okay, I pick up my phone and see a text that came in about forty minutes ago. It's just past midnight now.

GABRIEL: #whiteflagemoji

"Yeah." I hear the relief in my voice. "Yeah, I'm good."

I break promises pretty often.

Not on purpose. It's mostly because half the time, when I make the promises (to myself, or other people, doesn't really matter who), I'm in survival mode. Being a Black kid does not leave you with a lot of value or utils to barter. So you promise shit you know your ass can't deliver on.

I hear my mother's voice in my head. *Don't write checks your ass can't cash.*

So, needless to say, I don't prioritize school over my bees. I try to, at first.

That lasted, oh, I don't know, all of twelve hours.

Luckily, I make it to my second day of college classes on time. And though this first one's at 11:00 a.m. and not early as all who-knows-what like Coco's, I'm still taking the W.

I meet Gabriel at one of SFSU's many vendor locations, a coffee shop called Café 101, which seems like lazy branding if you ask me.

Wish I could say it was by design, but I get there before he does. Which, for me, isn't ideal because then I get all dumb and nervous and start thinking up random scenarios involving us—I celeb-named us, too: *Torriel.* Doesn't it sound like some kind of angel that's been cast from heaven?—and that's not conducive to, like, *annnnything.* Because he's attached, and so am I. To LA. To the bees. To the very same place that never ceases to feel like both my vice and my savior.

But aside from all the catastrophizing I do, it turns out that arriving first and getting to watch him arrive has a pretty large payout.

He smiles the second he sees me, and it's weird because I was so stressed out that I somehow wouldn't recognize him or he wouldn't recognize me and then we'd just be these two completely unintentional Catfished dudes who no longer look like our social media photos but still think we do.

But that's not for London. Gabriel. Gabe.

He strides through the student marketplace like he is meant to, pivoting his head only a fraction to seek me out before, boom, finding me.

And he lights up.

And he seems relieved?

And he is coming toward me.

And he does not say a word. He pulls his canvas bag up and over his head to take it off and when he does, his T-shirt rides up a little, though he quickly pulls it down, like, way rougher than he needs to, as though he's self-conscious about it.

About his happy trail. Or maybe—maybe—he's self-conscious about how happy his happy trail makes me.

Food for thought, food for thought.

"I didn't think you'd recognize me," he says. And his voice kicks the crap out of my ability to function. Until he reaches up and deftly ties his mane of multicolored hair up into this thing on top of his head, sliding the tie on his wrist around it without a single thought.

Probably something he does all the time. He'd have to. His hair is long as sin.

But in my head, it's a miraculous thing. The way his arms, toned with the kind of muscle that couldn't have existed in eighth grade, push up and pull, to complete a seemingly simple, completely mundane task. He's all sinew and lean muscle, and my goodness—ass!

The ass on that boy.

Okay wait, sorry. We're back online.

"You okay?" he says. "Did I sit down at the wrong table? Are you not Torrey Mac?"

I laugh. It's this huge, obnoxiously farm-animal thing. "No one's called me that since middle school. But yeah. It's me. Fleshy and all that mess."

His smile is quiet, and I like the way his eyes turn into these tiny slits displaying his lashes like a fan.

"You want coffee or something? Tea? Smoothie?"

"They have too many options here."

"I was really about to say that." He fiddles with a second tie that's still around his wrist.

Gabe crosses an ankle over his knee as the barista comes to our table. He has another tie around his ankle. How many does one person need? Jesus Christ.

I realize suddenly that I am staring too long at his ankles. But I'm not even sure I can help it. I can see them perfectly as his foot bounces up and down, his seen-better-days Vans just dancing. He's got a huge vein that runs up the top of his foot and the tiny, light brown hairs visible, peeking out of the bottom of his tight black jeans, are somehow incredibly sexy.

This is not me. This is not who I am.

I mean. With Gabe. Back then. It was a month. Two months. Not even—fifty-nine days to be exact.

Alright, fine. We were inseparable for an entire school year, through seasons and growth spurts. So maybe at first it *felt* like fifty-nine days, the way they skipped past us and didn't look back. But it was so much more.

He felt like my everything that year. My only thing.

He orders hot black coffee, and I almost die of laughter. "You are so predictable, when did you become a college fuckboy?"

"You're one to talk, Mr. I-Lift-Girls-Over-My-Muscular-Ass-Shoulders-and-Post-the-Pics-to-Instagram."

"Wow. So you've been stalking me?"

He looks at me like I'm crazy, lifting his hot black tar in a cup to his lips. He talks as he blows just over the lip of his cup to cool it off. "Of course I have. You're not the only one who got kinda lost after that whole thing in eighth grade."

That whole thing in eighth grade. I really don't even know how to talk about it. So I resolve not to. I guess that's a pretty okay thing to refer to it as. A Whole Thing.

"Who says I was lost?" I counter. I scramble a little bit, thinking I've killed *the mood.*

He only offers back a sedate "Mm," brows raised, lips clipped to his coffee mug.

"So, how'd you end up here? Back in California. And enrolled here at SFSU. That was a shocker."

"The universe has jokes." But he doesn't elaborate on that particularly vague thing, switching instead to, "Do anything fun since you got here?"

I waffle. But in the end, I skip over the billion-dollar burritos with CAKE and the mandatory "Welcome" thing with Desh, et cetera. "Not really. I'm kinda stuck on what's back home."

"Thought you hated home."

"I do. I did. I mean, I do but there are parts . . . my bees."

Scale of one to ten, ten being LMAO YOU DUMBASS, how much of a dumbass do I sound like right now?

"Bees?" Gabriel says.

"It's a long story."

"So shorten it for me." He shrugs, like it's so easy to shorten the longest love affair of my life.

"Okay, well. For his royal highness, I'll try. Basically, I own an apiary."

"Which is . . . what, exactly? You know, not for me. But for the idiots in the back."

"Right. Yes. The idiots. An apiary is essentially a bee farm. A place to keep bees. To farm honey and breed more bees. Especially ones like the Hawaiian yellow-faced bee." He's quiet. I elaborate, "They're on the endangered species list?"

"Wow," he says. "Yeah, wow. I never knew."

"Most people don't. And I never told anyone about the farm. It wasn't always mine though."

"No?" he says.

"No." And I *don't* provide more there. Seems to be the name of the game, and right now I'm down to play it. "So you're trying to do some kind of arts major? What, like, art history?"

He looks like the type. An artist.

"Nah," he says, a shy grin on his face. A shy grin I've never seen before. I like it so much on him. "Dance. It's an arts major and a dance focus."

Dance. I don't think I remember that.

"Yeah, the look on your face says you don't recall that. You probably wouldn't remember because I didn't let my mom push it on me outside of the dance community. You know how brown moms are. I loved it. And still do. But it was hard to be a brown boy named London who had an attraction to dance and also had a similar thing going with dudes part-time."

"Got that Afro-Brazilian wave going, she doesn't play."

"I'm saying. She will kill my ass over something trivial. I love her, though, that's my woman."

"So . . . dance. Can I ask what kind of dance?"

This one. Look, look! You see it? That crinkled-nose smile? Probably number two on my favorites list.

"You? Of course. You can ask me anything."

Dangerous, that word. Anything.

Once, back then, he and I snuck out. It wasn't too late, but just dark enough that we felt like we'd managed something big, half walking, half running from bus stop to bus stop and then, finally, breathless, landing on some random suburb's almost-tidy corner.

"What should we do now?" I asked.

"Anything," he whispered right into my ear. And I swear I felt his lips brush my neck. There and then gone, just like the boy himself would be mere weeks after that.

Gabriel continues, "Lyrical. Contemporary." He doesn't do that thing a lot of people do when they talk about their talent where they shrug or get shy or downplay it. He owns it. Leans back all long torso, ropy arms, and delicate fingers, red at the knuckle.

He's proud of himself, but he's also got pride in the craft, too. You can tell by the way he lights up.

"Wow," I say. "That's amazing."

"You know what contemporary dance is?"

"No," I say, a genuine smile attacking my face, trying to fight for the maximum amount of space.

He has to compose himself before he can continue. "Yeah, a lot of people don't. If it's not ballet, hip-hop, or salsa, it's new news. Which is funny, because contemporary-lyrical dance is basically a mixture of all those things."

"Lyrical dance . . . set to song lyrics?"

Gabriel snaps his fingers and then points at me. "Precisely. Lyrical and contemp are basically the same things. The only difference is that lyrical's choreography relies more on the lyrics of the song. Contemp is about the nonverbal feeling you get. About which ancestor living inside you shakes your frame the most."

"You like that one best."

"You're right on that," he says. "What about you? I would attempt to guess what direction you're headed in but you're sort of an enigma, Torrey McKenzie."

He reaches one arm across his body to scratch his biceps, which then turns into his thumb pressing into the skin there, casually moving back and forth.

I can't stop staring at it. "I'm really not. I'm undecided."

"Keeping your options open."

"Not really. Just kind of wondering what my options are at this point."

He's so quiet right before he says, abruptly, "Torrey, do you go to church?"

And I don't really know where he's going with this so I answer with no hesitation. "Uh, church? I don't know, my fam's pretty serious about it."

"Okay, but, like, do you go to church?"

I get what he's saying now.

"Kind of. Yeah. I sometimes need to believe in something bigger than me."

He nods.

"Why?"

"I just . . . I just find myself wanting to know things about you. Needing to know things about you."

Kind of heavy for a just-coffee type of thing. But the rest of it. God.

He scratches the skin just below his lip. There's a tiny patch of hair there that gives way to the patch of it on his chin. Those two puzzle pieces go well with his mustache, which, somehow, I'm just now noticing, too. Dudes and our facial hair—it's all totally contrived, trust me. All for attraction purposes. We plan this stuff, meticulously.

But still, his facial hair, the hair on his arms, and the fine strands on his legs, between the end of his jeans hem and that damn ankle . . . it's the ideal balance. There-but-not-furry.

"I'm kind of a heathen, so anytime I get within twenty-five feet of a religious institution, I set flames to the building as well as any small children present."

"Yikes. Not the kids, Gabe. Oh, no."

"Oh, yes," he says. "The kids, Torrey."

I'm laughing and trying to hold most of it in so I don't seem overeager when he says, "They say it's supposed to get easier."

"What is? Going to church?"

"Figuring out who you want to be."

My eyes hold his for a moment. Or his eyes hold mine. I'm not sure which, but eventually it ceases to matter.

11.

Emery Grymchan—the E in our lovely CAKE acronym— is all gaming consoles, elitist anime preferences, and horror manga. Her skin, the most entrancing umber brown I've ever seen, plus the sunburst of black beachy waves around her head automatically shove her in the category of Cooler Than Torrey McKenzie.

She and I share a class, it turns out. (Remember that 11:00 a.m. Tuesday class I was on time to? Yeah, turns out it's twice a week, and I missed the Thursday lecture. So here I am, a week after that. The professor does not let this go unnoticed.)

"Nice of you to join us for both classes this week, Mr.

McKenzie," he says. Dr. Che is a brown man living his best gay life, lipstick and highlights kicking ass. (Yes, I know what highlighter is. Aunt Lisa used to practice using it on me. She only stopped when Theo started to make comments about me and animal testing.)

I slide in, not quietly, next to Emery, who has her massive sack full of probably small babies and eighteen copies of *1Q84* saving my seat.

Settled, laptop on my desk, book out, highlighter, pencil, perfect I'm-listening-I'm-learning student face in play, I nudge Em.

"Ow! What?" she hisses.

I nod at her laptop and mouth Facebook.

So she opens her web browser and navigates to your granny's favorite form of social media, where I have messaged her.

TM: I remembered something interesting about you the other day

EG: About me? What??

TM: The Collective, out in Oakland and down through LA— don't you basically stan for them eternally?

EG: OK yes, so if you'll recall, stanning for The Collective is the reason I have an arrest record

TM: I know I know, just hear me out

EG: And that I am firmly entrenched in this life where I follow all the rules and all the laws

TM: Emery.

EG: And that I need to keep my head low to the ground now if I wanna keep DREAMing, iykwim

Emery and her family came here from Senegal a couple of years back.

TM: I do. And listen. None of what I need from you here is gonna be illegal. I just need info, resources, maybe a slap on the ass so that I don't fall behind on anything.

EG: You're already behind in this class, Torr

TM: I am?

TM: Or, I mean, I know, but that doesn't even matter

TM: I'm talking about getting behind on whatever paper trail is gonna help me keep my bees

EG: What do you eman DOESN'T MATTER

EG: *mean

TM: I EMAN I'm not staying here. I'm gonna disenroll, I'm going down to admissions soon to figure out what I gotta do.

EG: Torr. I hate to tell you, but that's gonna be a PITA. My cousin Roger did that. They made him pay back, like, all of his fin aid.

My stomach drops. Dr. Che screams something about fact-checking and investigative journalism. Literally, he screams. He's super passionate about fact-checking.

Anyway, the point is his shouting resonates.

It's a mirror of just how wrecked I feel right now. I've already used a good chunk of my grant, and I really don't want to have to take out any loans.

If I leave outright, it'll mean I'm doing so willingly, failing each and every one of my classes. Which means my GPA would drop lower than Desharu's postpubescent balls. It'd be nonexistent and that would make it all but impossible to reapply or even reenroll here at SFSU later. If there ever is a later.

The smart choice—the only choice, off top—is to get in there before that Add/Drop deadline.

But leaving . . . it feels like the only way to pick up all those broken pieces at home. It feels like the only way to hold on to Uncle Miles, to thank him, to keep him alive and make him proud.

What am I even doing? Everything in my life is falling apart. I swallow repeatedly, hoping I don't choke on my tongue or something and screw that up, too. I'm not ready. I don't know how the hell I made it this far, to a university in a city that isn't the Hills, alone. Who do I even think I am trying to keep my apiary from drowning when I can't even keep my own head above choppy waters?

My favorite thing about Uncle Miles was probably his sense of style. He took huge amounts of pride in that, and he taught me to do the same thing for myself. I can remember being a kid and having this super-intense desire to be just like him.

It wasn't even a hard thing to do. Uncle Miles and I have always looked a ton alike. Our baby pictures are near identical, always the butt of every easy joke at the family reunion. Even now that I'm older, I'd still wager I could pass for Uncle Miles. Both dark skinned with similar builds, rangy arms and legs, sinew, song and struggle deep in the bones. Deep-set brows settled onto angular foreheads. Too-full mouths pressed into sharp jaws.

The lashes—not gonna lie, girls have a thing for the lashes. Never did me any good, but gave Uncle Miles plenty of play.

And the hair. Uncle Miles always said we shouldn't ever be caught without a fade, so I try to make sure I stick to that. A shadow taper every couple of weeks while the top dances on a twist of its own. Which reminds me, I guess I need to try and find a freaking barber in this white-ass college town, then?

It's weird, this fundamental peer isolation. Living in a town where I'd have to *seek out* a barbershop with barbers of color and not just waltz into the first Great Clips I see on the corner. It's new and, you know, it kind of leaves the door open for the sort of exploration I'm not sure I'm ready for.

As I approach, there's a guy at the entrance of my dorm talking to one of our RAs, Kiana. Dude looks familiar. He's dressed like a shark. I immediately don't like him and his greasy, slicked-back, probably dyed blue-black hair.

Aim for that, Torrey.

For what?

His money. You need to aim for that one day. That success.

Man, money ain't everything.

Lookit you, kid. Money ain't everything. That's for damn sure. But ain't his suit fresh?

Uncle Miles and I used to have conversations just like that all the time. One of his main lessons was making sure I was reaching high enough and not selling myself short.

Now, I pat Kiana's arm the minute I make it over to them—a gesture that says, *Hey! There are witnesses and so trying to kidnap people from here won't go well for you, Random White Man.*

I'm about to squeeze my way past the pair when dude says, "You're Torrey."

"Who's asking."

The guy smirks. He's new money. Clean money. Money my part of the hood doesn't see on a visit and definitely not on any long-term kind of fly-in. But this isn't the Hills, is it.

"I'm not asking. I remember you."

"Can I help you?"

He laughs, and I place my hands on my hips and stand in front of Kiana in the world's worst example of male chauvinism I've ever seen.

Kiana intones, "Torr?"

"Can I help you?" I say again, ignoring Kiana. She doesn't walk away though, even if being here's not in her job description, but that's what I've figured out about her. She'll back you one hundred even if she's not required to. Though, usually it's like, she won't rat you out for co-ed after-hours junk or she'll come unlock the door for you if you're shwasted and getting back to the dorm after 11:00 p.m. or whatever.

"My name's Rick. Richard Mathew, but Rick."

"Pretty sure 'Dick' is supposed to be short for Richard."

"Yes," he says, lips pursed. I take that as a win, point to me. Asshole. "I think you know why I'm here."

"Can't say that I do. Which is why I've asked you twice what I can do for you. As you can see, I'm kinda busy being a college student here and Kiana doesn't have all day to entertain you either."

"Yeah. Well, you'll have a lot more time to be a busy college student with Kiara here after you hear me out."

Kiara. What a jackass.

He continues, "I'm the reason you're going under."

I feel all the fight drain out of me. I'm not even entirely sure what it is he's saying. And yet still, it's like being unplugged. Like water draining out of a bathtub.

He continues, "I just came by to get some insight into who you are and how we might be able to help each other."

Kiana whispers, "This doesn't feel like an okay thing, Torr."

I nod in her direction then continue to Dick Richard. "I see."

"Yeah. This's been years in the making. I remember meeting your uncle. What's his name, uh . . . ?"

"Miles."

"That's it!" He snaps. "Your uncle Mike, he—"

"That wasn't at all subtle, I literally just told you his name. It's Miles. I'd appreciate you not pulling that one again." The whites—always on some bull like this.

"Yeah, sure sure. Anyway, I was real sorry to hear about what happened with him. But your space. It's a dream. Been hearing what they got planned for that neighborhood, and I'm telling you—you kids are gonna love it."

"Oh?" I'm giving him a whole lotta fuck-you face right now, and he's not picking up on it at all. Maybe because he's barely talking to me. It's more of a talking-at-me type of thing. Again—that's white people.

This is for y'all. No, no—not you, Black and brown folk.

The whites do it unconsciously. And so I get it. But that still doesn't make it cool.

Oh. Wow, yes. Okay. You—A White—think you're not complicit in this? Very cute. Very false.

This is what we call a *microaggression.*

So you've got The Whites who don't realize they're doing it, and then there are the rest—the Woke Whites—who believe that they're above it.

You're not, Cheryl-Rose. You're not. All those callout threads you do on the Twitter dot com, you're not exempt from them.

To me, it's important to understand that these are learning opportunities.

"Yeah, we're talking strip malls and parks and lash bars and—"

"Listen, Dick. I'm sorry you've wasted your time here. But I'm not taking this news with my ass planted on a seat. I'm appealing."

He scoffs. Like, for real, it is a scoff.

Only white people scoff.

"I know. How do you think I found you? Personal information in a Facebook group? Really? Plus, appeals never work."

"Yeah, well. Let's hope for the sake of you and your plans that it doesn't. Because I've got plans of my own for the place, and those plans don't include you or whatever the hell the city has planned."

Plans plansplansplansplanswtftorreyplansplans—

"I see," he says.

We're both quiet a second, neither willing to concede until—"Torrey!"—someone else calls my name. I hear Kiana exhale a sigh of relief behind me, like she just couldn't wait for this exchange to be over.

I flash a toothy smile at Mr. Dick, adjust the glasses on my nose, and feign confidence with all the bravado I've gathered in my eighteen years as a Black male on this planet.

"Duty calls," I say.

He hands me his business card. And I take it because I am a moron.

"See you soon," is all he gives me back before he walks away.

That oily, scummy, Russian mob–looking ass headass is going to push me over the edge. I feel it already.

"Torrey!"

But I pack all that away—just like I always do, just like I'm good at—and focus on the next fire that needs putting out: the amount of Psych 101 catch-up discussion-board posting I'm in for.

*O*ne of the reasons I decided to go to school here in San
Francisco is because of a woman called Patricia McKenzie.

Patricia McKenzie is the fifty-six-year-old mother of one.
Patricia McKenzie worked as a registered nurse for twenty-two
years. Patricia McKenzie was stealing prescription drugs from
her employer for half that amount of time.

Patricia McKenzie is in a medically induced coma and has
been for five years.

I was thirteen when it happened. I knew she was sick long
before she did. The pill bottles, the mood swings, the despera-
tion. Not even the amount of love she tried to smother me with

could disguise that. But still, she loved her medical meth more. More than me, more than her job and her family. More than anything. And I was okay with that because as much as she could give anyone—she gave me the most of her.

Patricia McKenzie resides at God Willing Hospice Care. It's pricey as hell. The apiary's profits have actually paid for a lot of what her costs constitute. Medicaid pays for the rest. There are still times when I wonder if Theo will ever help me.

He says he's ready to get rid of her. She's broken because she's been dependent on prescription drugs for more than half my life, and I'm broken as a result of that.

In Theopolis McKenzie's mind, bad parenting equals the reason gay-ass kids are gay. Aka, a problem. I've had the "homophobia in the Black community" chat with Theo enough times to know that he's an old dog you *can* teach new tricks to, but his stubborn ass won't learn them.

The air is so much fresher in San Francisco. I know part of it is because it's all but sitting on water and half the city isn't basically just a dust bowl the way LA is.

I feel a breeze climb up the back of my shirt as I enter the hospice center. The place smells clinical. Like someone dropped a giant-ass vial of insulin and didn't clean it up. (It's happened to Lisa enough for me to know exactly what that smells like.) The walls are throw-up-your-Pepto-on-my-raw-piece-of-salmon pink and in desperate need of a long overdue face-lift. It's quieter than I think it should be. It's always been that way. I feel like, when you walk into a place like this, you shouldn't be able to hear the thoughts that are running through your head like child looters straight out of some *American Horror Story* plot.

The desk is almost as tall as I am. I press up close against it.

"Hi, Torrey here to see Patricia McKenzie."

The woman at the counter finally looks up. "Sign in," she says, pointing. "You know the way."

And I do. I've been here enough times to know. A handful, maybe. Probably less. Truth is, three trips to this place would still feel like a thousand. Too many.

The trips I spent coming here, on the Greyhound and the MTA, as young as thirteen years old, expedited the time it would have taken me to grow up. Thirteen is too young to be traveling a distance like that by yourself. But for her, I did.

This is a place I'll never forget, even after she's long gone and these halls have forgotten me.

I catch a spare glimpse of the e-reader on the sign-in desk, spotting a few lines of the book the receptionist is reading and look away so quickly. Jesus.

Delilah Fisher, whoever you are, you're the world's filthiest author, and you've scarred me for life in about eight or nine words. Congrats.

A drug called Dextropropoxyphene is the reason we're here today. I mean, not here on Earth here. Just, like, in this shitty care center.

It's the reason Moms is here, too. Don't get me wrong—her use of the drug started as an entirely innocent thing. Workplace injury resulted in the need for a mild pain medication. From there, her inability to work, her inability to, thusly, pay the bills, and then her need to move in with Theo, pushed her headlong into a love affair with depression and non-medical-grade Dexedrine.

It's like meth. It's basically methamphetamine prescribed by people who spend hundreds of thousands of dollars on school, just to one day be able to give it to you.

It's the reason Moms got sloppy getting out of the shower one day. The reason she slipped, hit her head, and would not have suffered a TBI—unless she was already on an extreme amount of ding-ding-ding, what'da we got for 'em, Johnny? You guessed it, methamphetamines. A drug, when used for a long-enough duration of time and at an excessive-enough frequency, has the potential to swell the brain even without a clumsy shower spill.

So really, I'm sure her falling and me finding her was just a little something extra God slapped in there for me.

Lisa would kick my ass for blaspheming.

While most patients in the care center have rooms that are decorated in mementos, family photos of their dogs and ugly grandkids, Moms's room is as sparse as it was the day she was moved in here. Would've been up to me to put up some pics or even just mail them to be tacked onto the room's standard-issue corkboard, but I didn't.

Having a bunch of family photos that don't include her or family photos of her dead brother or family photos of, I don't know, me—that kind of thing isn't palatable. Not for me and not for Moms either. At least, not for the version I knew.

Inside, there's the bed—hospital grade—and an end table. There's a pitcher for water, which I'm pretty sure hasn't ever been used. Not by me. Definitely not by Moms. There's a dresser where clothes and things should go. Moms cycles in and out of the same five or six sleeping gowns and that's about it. No need for dresser drawers or anything resembling them. In the farthest corner of the room is another chair, the upholstery on which can be described as tweed's older, uglier third cousin. There's an ass indent in the middle of the chair so deep it might be mistaken for a moon crater, and the honey-brown wooden arms seem to have been attacked by some very aggressive toddler's teeth.

Still, though it's probably ridden with germs and the ghost of butts past, it's where I sit every time I'm here.

The farthest seat. Because as much as I like to tell myself I'm a good son for continuing to visit her, I'd really rather I not be. So, a "happy" medium is me keeping as much distance as I can between me and the elephant/comatose body in the room.

Schrödinger's Torrey.

Nelly the Nurse, as I call her—her name really is Nelly and she is a nurse—checks in on me twice. The way I figure it, she's got an every-thirty-minutes-check-on-Torrey schedule running.

Luckily for her, I never stay more than about an hour, hour and fifteen tops.

That doesn't change now just because I live locally. I'm out of there the second it feels like I've paid my dues.

By the time I get back on my bus to SFSU, the tremor in my hands is gone.

*G*abriel's favorite activity is running his long-fingered hands through his hair. He has a lot of it. Even though 50 percent of the time it's trapped in some complicated up-thing (Clarke calls it a topknot). But so, it probably stands to reason that my obsession with him has to do with how many times a day he takes it down and puts it back up with the dexterity of someone who's had what I would call *an exorbitant amount* of hair all their life.

"You've so much hair," I say. We're sitting right outside one of the three campus food halls, both picking at some fusion food–type dish, like stir-fry noodles, pizza toppings, and other things that shouldn't go together but do. Or, in Gabe's case, french fry shawarma—a thing that should go together and, yes, actually does. Give it a try.

"You've so much hair," he counters.

"No, not compared to you."

He shrugs. He's always been so damn nonchalant about his hair when it's always just had this ability to drive me wild. "My hair is a lot in that it's just long. Yours is a lot in that it's lush and thick as hell. I'm jealous."

"Don't be."

His lips come to the bottle of Jarritos in his hand in a way that should probably be rated something above PG-13. "I'd kill for this to be something other than soda."

I grunt and shove a marinara-coated piece of broccoli into my mouth. It's quiet until I look up and realize he's staring at me.

"What?"

"Nothing," he says.

"No. Not nothing." That look doesn't say nothing. "What?"

"Torrey, do you drink?"

Okay. Hello, left field. "Uhh . . . on purpose?"

"I feel like the answer could just be a yes or a no?" He laughs.

Setting my plastic fork down gently, I clear my throat. "I mean, it's not that I don't drink. I could, I guess. I just haven't."

"Ever?"

"Haven't," I clarify. "So, have not. Ever. Yeah."

"Wow."

"Wow?"

"Wow."

I push my fork around my plate a little more before I realize I'm not eating this nightmarish plate of food anymore and didn't really enjoy any of it to begin with.

"I didn't take you for the type," he says.

"The type? The type of what?"

He shrugs, wipes up some of the sauce on his plate with a folded French fry. "Straight edge. You weren't all innocent like that back when I knew you."

"I don't know how to respond to that."

"You don't have to."

"Don't I?"

"Do you?"

"I hate it when you do that," I say. Truth is, I don't. Feels like an intimate game of thumb war, only with words and eye contact that lasts just a little bit too long.

"It's not on purpose that I don't drink or haven't or any of that. Just, you know, with all the shit going on at the apiary—I gotta keep a clear head. My mind's pretty focused on what my next steps will be. How I'll handle all this from so far away. I need to figure out what I'm going to do before the Add/Drop deadline."

Every day, the university sends out an automated email to the entire student pop, reminding us how close the Add/Drop date is. Eleven days. The reminder sends a wave of quiet panic rippling through my system, the spiraling thoughts and physical mirror of them, a reminder that my life is not my own.

He's quiet, stares at me but says nothing.

I need to fill the silence. "I'm a mess. If I don't figure something out, I'll have to leave and go back there. I'm stressing hard, and I feel like I'm losing. There's some guy, he approached me the other day with Kiana. Like, he straight up came to my dorm to talk to me about how he was basically gonna run me from my farm. Like, on the real, it felt like a threat. It was a threat. I'm just trying to handle business and being wasted isn't part of that."

Finally, Gabe nods. "You think too much."

"I—what?"

He stands so abruptly I almost fall backward in my chair from the force of his ejection.

"Let's go," he says. "You need to just . . ." He makes this wild gesture with his hands that I *think* means loosen up?

He's up and walking out the door a moment later, all but demanding I follow. So I do, thick glasses pushed all the way up the bridge of my nose, plate of horrible fusion food in hand and then, as I'm walking out the door, into the nearest garbage.

He drags us to a dive bar called High Tide located a block just before we hit a section of town called the Tenderloin, a gritty, half-hopeless, half-technicolor neighborhood known for both its speakeasies and also its tendency toward crime. SFSU spent no time telling students about this area during orientation. They painted it in what I think was supposed to be a dark light, if that makes any sense. But for me, all I heard was that it never gentrified along with the rest of the city.

There's really not a lot that's special about it, which if you ask me, makes it pretty special. There's a lot of glitz and glamour in Los Angeles, and it's here in San Francisco, too.

So, occasionally, it's nice to see something that's basic. Easy. Simple.

It's still pretty early in the evening. Not a ton of people in this struggle box of a dive bar, just Gabe and I plus two other groups of three and a couple of solo drinkers who seem like they've seen their prime twice over.

Seated at the counter, Gabriel turns on, his smile going up a few extra watts, mouth sliding long across his face, eyelashes just ready to put you in a daze. He does that all in the space of a few seconds, and the bartender seems to notice.

"Hey, man," Gabriel says. "Can we get four shots of tequila and two pints of whatever you have on tap?"

"Kind of tequila?" the guy says, not even bothering to card us. He doesn't even look up from the glass he's "cleaning."

That rag is filthy.

"I don't care," Gabe says. "Whatever's cheap."

The bartender's eyebrows go up as if to say, you sure?

Gabriel laughs. "Whatever's cheapest," he confirms. "We're not choosy."

The bartender does a jerky chin-chuck-nod and goes off to get our bevy of alcohol, which I hope is mostly for Gabe because holy shit.

"You've done this a lot," I say.

He turns to me and pulls out his wallet and debit card, sliding it across the bar. "Yeah."

The bartender pulls on the beer tap lever like he hates it. "Close it out?"

"Keep it open."

And then Gabriel's grabbing the shots in his hands. "Grab those," he says, nodding at the two sweating glasses of beer.

I don't know whether to be afraid of the smile that's on his face or . . . turned on by it?

"Have you done this before?" he says, divvying up the shots. "Right, what am I saying? Of course you haven't. Okay," he says, and then lifting a finger with each word he continues, "It's lick, tequila, lime. Got it?"

"Salt, poison, fruit, yeah, I got it."

He licks his wrist and pours a little salt on his first and then, after I lick my own, mine. "I promise the poison won't matter to you after the first two."

"There's going to be more than two?"

He chuckles.

You ever sniff a habanero pepper a little too closely?

Good, don't. Chances are, you've at least experienced something similar if you can recall your first time with a shot of tequila. Although, the words *shots* and *tequila* do not lend themselves to solid memory.

So anyway, then we're going and—he is right!—I don't care about annnnything after that.

"Wow, you really haven't done this whole teenage-drinking thing then, have you?"

I look up from my inspection of the probably empty shot glass. Why do they call it a shot glass? Why not just, like, tiny glass or miniature cup?

Why does the shot cup seem empty but not actually look empty?

He takes the glass out of my hand and laughs. He does not let go of my hand even though the miniature shot is no longer in it.

"No," I say to him. "I haven't." Then, "My lips are a little bit numb. I think."

"After two shots? Wow. I love lightweight drinkers."

"You get a lot of people drunk on their first go with alcohol?"

I like the way he licks his lips after taking a pull on his beer. "Just you," he says.

Kind of liking that, too.

My body feels like a lo-fi beat.

"Why are my lips numb?"

"One of two reasons. A: too much, too fast."

"That one," I say. "Bet you it's that one!"

He laughs. "Or, well, there is B: You are mildly allergic to alcohol."

"Cool!" I say. But really, I'm not sure why that comes out. Being allergic to alcohol is decidedly less cool than anything else.

He shakes his head. He thinks I am hopeless. Newsflash to you and him: I am hopeless.

"Why haven't you had alcohol? You know, before you were responsible for the apiary and all that. Hard to believe your family kept all that stuff under supreme lock and key."

"Nah," I say, taking a long, heavy gulp off my beer. It tastes like earwax? "I just didn't feel like I could drink."

"I don't follow."

Yeah, most people wouldn't. "Hard to feel okay about getting drunk when you're too busy taking care of people who depend on you to pick up their slack."

If I wasn't taking care of bees, I was taking care of people. Adults.

Moms. Uncle Miles. Even Theo at one point depended on me to make sure the utility checks didn't bounce and bill collectors didn't catch him unawares by calling at inopportune times. And then when Uncle Miles died, there was a point when all I wanted to do was forget, but the bees. The apiary. Someone had to take care of that for him, and he chose me.

And Lisa chose me, too. Chose me to lean on. To make sure she ate and smiled at least once a day and spoke out loud to someone on occasion.

And me—I didn't have nobody to lean on. So how was I supposed to lean on any kind of substance? No room for any of that.

"You any good at pool?" I say.

"I'm alright. You think you can beat me at a game of pool while you're this pissed?"

I know I can. "I don't know. Probably."

And it turns out I do several things very well while I'm so drunk that my mouth goes numb.

I beat Gabriel at two games of pool, and then proceed to school two other dudes, too. The last game I play, Gabriel manages to put a number on it, and we end up winning forty bones off the dude after I sink my last solid.

For most of my life, Moms and I went to church every Sunday. Never missed a service. And for most of that time, she made me sing with the kids' choir because "Baby, God ain't give you this talent so you could hide it. He gave you that voice so you could honor Him with it."

I don't karaoke so much as belt out some oldies that Gabe puts on the jukebox. Two women twice my age come up to me and tell me my voice is beautiful. One of them is bold enough to stroke my chin and then covertly-but-not-at-all-covertly touch my lips that I still can't feel because I've now had two more shots—vodka this time!

Gabriel, when I asked for something that is not tequila, protested and told me that I wouldn't love myself tomorrow.

I almost tell him that it's not a huge difference from how I feel about myself today. But I don't. I just down the vodka—worse than the tequila!!!!—and keep singing and keep playing pool and keep telling random strangers that I think this place is where I'm meant to be.

Don't remember a lot after that. What I do remember is Gabriel's arm around my waist as we walk home. I remember thinking about how hilly the streets of San Francisco are. I remember Gabriel pressing his forehead into my shoulder while we sat and waited on a bench at the BART station.

The last thing I register is me being handed off from Gabriel, who smells like shampoo, to Desh, who smells like AXE body spray.

My bed smells like honey. Like home. Like bees and heavy heartbeats and remembering.

At next class, Coco is not in her office when I arrive at 6:56 a.m.

She's also not in her office at 6:59 a.m. or 7:05 a.m. or 7:17 a.m. or 7:33 a.m.

At which point, I take the elevator downstairs. And see her. Sitting at one of the tables near the coffee cart. Reading the paper.

"Is this for real right now."

Coco lowers her newspaper, which I notice is actually just the campus paper. Campus newspapers don't count. I mean, I know I've only been a college student for like two minutes, but it just feels like a fact that should be true given it's produced by the generation that thinks it's cool to wear spinoff MAGA hats that say things like, "Make Journalism Gay Again."

Which isn't a sentiment I'm opposed to, so much as the train it arrives on.

"Is what for real?" Coco says.

"I was waiting upstairs outside your office. And you're just down here drinking coffee and reading the paper."

She pouts. Like, actually bottom-lip-out pouts and then says, "It's matcha."

"Can I go now."

The paper crumples in her small hands, and she tosses it into a nearby trashcan before pushing all her hair from one side of her head to the other. "I mean, you could. But class starts in twelve minutes. Might as well stick around." She kicks the chair out.

"I'm good, thanks." Translation: I'm good, luv. Enjoy.

"Sit down, Torrey." Translation: Sit. The fuck. Down.

She's giving me Aunt-Lisa-Eye so I do exactly what the hell she demands and I sit. And we spend several minutes in silence. She's laughing hysterically at her phone for the entire eleven and a half minutes we're there, and I just watch because anyone with that much hair on their head deserves an audience.

As we're walking back up to the lecture hall, she says, almost to herself, "Man, I love those YouTube Girl-Horse breakup videos."

Phone in hand, I go over the list of books Emery recommended I look into. *Fundamentals of Property Law*, Lance Freeman's *There Goes the 'Hood*, *Property Law for Dummies*, et cetera. She thought that third recommendation was comedic genius.

I make the fifteen-minute trek from dorms to campus library when I run smack dab (do people my age even say "smack dab" anymore? Never mind) into Gabriel.

"Whoa whoa whoa whoa. Where's the fire, McKenzie?" he says. Do people my age even say, "Where's the fire?" anymore? No. No, we do not. But Gabriel Silva makes it work.

"Um, the library?"

"Hey, something came up, I'll talk to you later," he says. And it's literally only then that I realize he's been holding a phone up to his ear.

I coast up on my toes and then back down. "You didn't have to do that."

He smiles. The most unnerving thing about Gabriel is that he doesn't rush his responses. Something I've known for a long time but have only recently come to appreciate.

A smile, light and airy and charming, touches his lips. "I know."

"Generally, girls who are your girlfriend don't enjoy abrupt hang-ups."

He pulls his hair down with several rough yanks and then twists it back up on the very top of his head. He's a mess. God, he's such a mess.

"Who says it was my girlfriend?"

"Wasn't it?" I say, eyebrow raised.

"If it was, would it be upsetting to you?"

Yes. "Should it be?"

"You tell me."

"What are we even talking about?"

He hitches his bag higher onto his shoulder. "I don't know, but I'm really into it."

Oof.

"Alright well. Now that I've filled your witty-retorts quota, I really do need to hit the library."

"Want company?"

"I do, actually."

The J. Paul Leonard Library is a five-floor glass monstrosity, and I love it. I've been in it a few times for my CIV class and have walked by it several times at night just because. It kinda reminds me of that movie *Anastasia*. All lit up and quiet, gold spilling across the outer walls, glass shining softly. I don't know. Sounds stupid, I guess. As a kid, I loved that movie, though. And my cousin Roger used to run around the yard at my auntie's house yelling to all the rest of the neighborhood kids, "Torrey in there watching Anesthesia again!"

I cried every time.

"You seem shocked," Gabriel says.

"What about?"

"Wanting company."

"Okay."

"Wanting my company?"

"I'm sorry," I say as we enter the elevators. "Was that a question?" First floor is where we'll find the online catalog computers.

I.

I will find the online catalog. Not we.

I.

"I don't have questions about anything, I know where I want to be."

My eyes roll so hard. "Yeah, the campus public library on a Friday night, apparently."

"Well," Gabriel says, "you're here."

"Yeah, but only because I have to be."

"No," he says, waiting for the elevator to bing and let us out. "I mean I want to be here. *Because* you are also here."

The doors slide open, and my insides do the same. A slow warmth fills my belly.

"Oh," I say. And that's literally it before I make my exit. I'm not trying to outpace him and practically run away like a fucking idiot, but that is exactly what I do.

"Someone's in a hurry to get some knowledge on."

"Property law."

"Property law? Not for a class then, I take it. Because no one studying property law is going to use this much energy rushing like the world's most eager beaver from the elevator toward a catalog of legal information. I bet—"

"You can't say stuff like that to me."

"I," he starts. "Oh, I . . . um. What?"

"That thing. About wanting to be here."

"Oh."

"Oh?"

Gabriel exhales. "Yeah, 'oh.' I just, I mean, I get it. Because I totally said that same thing to you. For the same reason." When I'd sent him that pic of Desh, wherein, I am in it. Not wearing a shirt.

"The same reason," I say. I can't say anymore than that though. Because *is it* the same reason? Is it really?

I think I understand, but I couldn't name it. Wouldn't ever. It just feels like admitting too much when there's no hope of reciprocation. Also, just. I'm not ready. I don't think I'm ready to call it anything. This wanting. This casual excitement.

I feel the wire connecting the computer's mouse to the modem and wrap it up-around-and-through my fingers, needing to do something with my hands.

"Yeah," he says. And he doesn't hesitate at all to add, "But I don't know if I can just not say anything to you about what kind of stuff is running through my head right now. Or running through my head all the time lately."

"Gabe."

"See?" he continues. He's not even getting really loud. His phone lights up in his hand, and he ignores it. "You just called me 'Gabe' and for some strange-ass reason, nobody ever calls me Gabe. And then you do. And I love it. I'm totally here for everything about your everything, and it's messing me up."

"I'm sorry," I say quietly. And I think I really am.

"God, Torrey. Don't be," he says. "Honestly, don't be."

Things happen so fast, I don't know how to catch them, wine glasses falling from high shelves, but he is here with me, surrounded by silent studiers sitting in front of their dedication to education, a soft hum that I think is being made by the lights in the vaulted ceilings, and he is looking at me, and he is promising me with that one look that

this boy is mine

and if my body felt anything but weightless, I'd be doing something about it. And you know what, it turns out to not even be necessary. Gabe—Jesus, Gabe—presses forward and my eyes are shut but I feel his lips brush the soft skin just below my earlobe as he whispers, "Mea culpa."

And my body experiences a shock of electricity so hot, the convulsions that rip through me have a sound wholly unique to themselves.

Also, my hand, tangled in the computer-mouse wire, jerks and the mouse, keyboard, and very nearly the modem, come crashing down.

I am mortified. People are staring. And I can't decide if it's at Gabriel or if it's at me. Probably me. Although, if it were Gabriel, I wouldn't blame a single soul. He's got this obvious comfort in his own body, and it makes me warm all over—a thing that has nothing to do with the embarrassment-blush I've got going as a result of having just taken down a university-issued desktop computer.

His posture straightens. "Shit!" It's loud enough to hit the very back of the stacks on this floor and also probably all the ones above it.

"Sorry!" I say to him. Don't know why. I just say it. Then I say it again to anybody who isn't wearing noise-canceling headphones. "I'm sorry. I'm going to go find some books now." Yes, Torrey, please continue to assault these people with your business.

I'm halfway down a row about Oregon state law when I notice Gabriel hanging back.

"Hey, I think I have to go," he says.

"Uh, yeah. Okay."

"I just realized I have to take care of something." A not-at-all-vague excuse.

"For sure. That's cool. Thanks for hanging in while I attempted to break the library's most valuable asset."

"Nah. Not the most valuable. They've got a ball autographed by Christy Mathewson up on the fifth floor near the *Sports Illustrated* section."

I don't know who she is, but sure. "Oh, dope."

He laughs and lick-bites his lip before saying, "See you around, McKenzie."

I check out six different books on property law, shove them all inside my backpack (to the dismay of every librarian in a fifty-mile radius) and decide I need to hunt down Emery. She is probably my number one resource at this point, given her connection to the Collective and its pro bono legal team. The Collective is Emery's home. They're her people. They're also extremely capable and accomplished on the social justice reform front.

There's no text back when I message to find out where she's at, but my first guess is correct. Everything's coming up Milhouse! (These days I take my wins where I can get 'em.)

And there she is. Center ring. Two French braids. Sports tank. Pink boxing gloves. And this steady look on her face that says nothing more than *Imma fuck you up*. It's so the opposite of how she normally is. All jittery-stuttery energy and video game graphic tees. Sunshine swimming just under her cheekbones, whereas now she's sporting some serious thunderstorm-warning clouds.

The gym is one story, not an incredibly large space. But I get the sense that it's just enough. Functional. Got people paired off, going at it, fists flying. Most are so in the zone they don't notice me walk in. Some notice me long enough to basically profile me and then discard me.

There's music blaring out of a large black speaker in one corner of the room. I pull my high school James Baldwin Academy crewneck off over my head and grip it in my fist as I walk closer to the ring Em is dancing around.

A shirtless guy in the ring with her bounces on the balls of his bare, tape-wrapped feet. Some white boy with black hair slicked over like he's Ryan Gosling's stunt double. I almost discount him until his circuit around the ring brings his face into my full view. He's got a gnarly scar across the bridge of his nose. I think for a second that it makes his mug kind of attractive, until he throws another punch at Emery and she ducks it, laughing. Kinda hard to worry about his piehole when his fists are capable of that anyway.

But Emery . . . oh, Emery.

Girl's a poem in the boxing ring. She's breathless. She's gorgeous. She's moving—dancing. She's a fire blazing in a rainstorm, a strike of lightning across a cornfield. She's everything.

"Jesus," I whisper. And it's like that one word breaks her focus. The spell is undone.

Her head jerks up, and she takes a direct hit right to the jaw. I flinch, but she barely does as her attention reverts back to its original target, and I get that this is her apiary. This is her good thing. Her pocket of solace.

She nails the other guy with a swift series of hummingbird jabs that he blocks and counters, her knee flies up to his gut then comes down as he stumbles back, but that's not a cue for her to retreat. No. She aims this hoppy, straight-legged kick right at him that catches his gut padding again, just like her knee did. A bell in the corner dings. Then, and only then, does she retreat, but not before she taps her gloves with his.

"Hey," she says with a smile. A pink mouthguard covers her

teeth, which she spits into a cup before saying, "What are you doing here?"

I shrug, hang on the ropes as she works at removing her gloves above me, and notice how cut her biceps are.

"I was in the neighborhood."

She rolls her eyes. "In the neighborhood from Prominski Hall? Doing what? This building is a fifteen-minute walk from the dorms, Torrey."

I hold my hands up, all, okay, you got me. "Shorter if you cut across the soccer field." I shrug. "I came to see you. Plus, I was at the library anyway. Shaves my time by like five minutes."

"Three." She holds out her gloves for me to undo the rest of the strings and ties.

It takes me longer to undo them than it likely would've taken her. "Alright, fine, wiseass."

"So, you came to see me. What for?"

Another shrug. Did it look super affected? I'm actually just trying to play it cool. I'm for sure the sunglasses emoji face right now, no? The smirk emoji is probably not far off, I can feel it. "I was hoping you might wanna do something? Hang out?"

All she says is "Mm." Just like a Black woman to give you an answer in less than a whole syllable.

My best smooth-boy smile in place, I help her out of the ring. (Because she tooooootally needed it. Sometimes I want to kick my own ass.) Uncle Miles and I used to have this theory that all dark-skinned Black boys have this one smile. The light skinneds do, too, but they lose it after like, I don't know, age twelve or whatever. I don't know, it's just science, I don't make the rules. Dark skin comes with a lot of fucked-up cons, but also some perks, too.

The Smoov Boy smile is one of 'em.

Although Emery isn't super receptive to it.

"Let's go," she says, slipping around me to grab her gym bag and cell phone. The giant case on it is Totoro, and I immediately respect Em a hundred times more for it.

As a kid I used to watch Studio Ghibli's shit all the time. *My Neighbor Totoro* was one we kept on repeat. Uncle Miles, quiet and focused in a way those films sort-of demand, used to sit and watch them with me whenever Moms and me would roll through. Theo always had something to say about it, a mumbled "girly-ass cartoons in my house" sort of sentiment.

I pretended not to hear them. I think Uncle Miles did, too, spinning the conversation to some loud-ass joke about how *My Neighbor Totoro* should have been *My Nigga Totoro*.

IMO, it fits much better.

The walk back to Prominski is actually fifteen minutes, like Emery says. But we stop to grab a coffee and then form some kind of unspoken agreement that we'll take our time getting back, measuring our steps slowly, like spoonfuls of sugar.

Emery lifts her coffee's lid and slurps some of the foam off the top. "We can meet with Ryan Q."

My already tight shoulders knot up just a little more and my stomach goes queasy. It occurs to me I've been consuming way too much caffeine and not enough actual food. There is just so much I have to do and so much I haven't done and where do I even start? The Add/Drop period is a mouthbreather standing too close right now. University's student email system does not let me forget that this thing is nine days away. Nine. I need to start making some moves. STAT.

"I can feel you panicking, Torrey."

I glance over at her. "I am. You're right. Who's Ryan Q? And what's the Q stand for?"

"You know," she says on a laugh, "I'm not sure. But no one has ever called him anything but Ryan Q or just Q, so that's the way we keep it. He's part of the Collective and basically manhandles all our legal junk."

An image of Emery being arrested comes to mind. She says it was during a peaceful protest that got reported by the locals who live in the community. There's a photo of it. It's her being dragged away by two white cops who are easily twice her size. Her mouth open, suspended on a permanent, silent scream.

I asked her once why she uses that photo as her profile picture. "Doesn't it just tell you who I am? That what I fight for has reduced me to this, and that I accepted." And I get it. I'm there, too, with the apiary.

Guard bees protect their hive and queen like soldiers. They emit a pheromone to warn the bees inside the hive of danger, usually at the cost of their own lives. Emery is kind of like that, too. A guard bee.

"So when can we meet him—Ryan Q?"

"Now, if you want. He lives out in Mojave Desert, but we can Skype him in my room."

"Yes, please. That one."

She laughs. "You gotta stop stressing."

Easier said than done. Somebody give Em a heads-up on that one.

"You're too young to be worrying this much. We are too young to be worrying this much. If working with the Collective has taught me anything, it's that things keep going. People keep trucking, and time keeps moving. All we can do is lead the line or follow it."

"Is this the equivalent of 'let the chips fall where they may?'"

She shrugs, letting us into her dorm room, where Clarke is sleeping, her laptop open in front of her playing an episode of what sounds to me like *Grey's Anatomy*.

"You could say that," Em mumbles. "Think my way was much more wisdom-y, though."

She grabs her laptop and then leads me out into the common area of their dorm suite. Dorm rooms like this house four to six students each. It's basically a mini apartment. Has its own bathroom and shower, its own kitchen, a common room situated right in the middle, and some even include balconies. Or maybe that's a rumor. Only the white students would know the real truth about that one.

Set up and ready to go, she pulls her phone out of her back pocket, gesturing for me to sit down next to her on the couch. This entire apartment smells like an apple cinnamon Glade PlugIn.

"I'm just gonna text Q to make sure he's free to Skype right now."

I hear the tiny *whoooop* sound that means the text's been sent. Not even a minute later, I hear the chime of an incoming text, which prompts Em to jump onto Skype.

Q looks like Moses.

Yep, biblical-ass Moses. I mean, do I know what the hell he *actually* looked like? No.

But have I seen *The Prince of Egypt*? Yes.

So work with me here. He looks like Moses.

He answers the audio/video call with a tight smile on his face, reserved and looking to all the world—i.e., Emery and myself—like he would rather be anywhere else.

"You look like you'd rather be anywhere else," she says.

Then and only then does he loosen, the space around his mouth going smooth.

It would only take half of half a brain to realize homedude is in love with Emery. Which, I mean. I don't know her exact orientation, but she seems pretty goddamn oblivious about it to me.

She pulls her shirt away from her body and sniffs the general armpit area a couple of times. Her face, scrunched up high for a moment, suggests she's satisfied enough with the hygiene there.

And see? The way she just stretched out long across the couch—face out of view of the camera, but Q . . . sprung. His eyes follow the rest of her appendages. Em? She's uninvested, picking at the chipped black paint on her nails, pushing her feet into my thigh—"Torrey, move, you're in my space!"—while the man on the screen scrambles to tamp his unruly, biblical hair down.

That's obliviousness, right? Or maybe that's just inexperience. Lord knows I can't read that kind of mess.

"I was in the middle of a cat nap before I hit my night job."

She glances at me. "Q works four different jobs, one of which is patrol at some fancy government agency rocket science space-ship company or whatever."

"Only about twelve percent of what she just said is true."

"Oh! This is Torrey, bee-tee-dub. Torr," she says, a bruised up hand in my direction, that goddamn foot *still prodding my leg* even though I'm only occupying one cushion and she's taking up two. "This is Ryan Q, passer of law school but somehow not the bar."

Ouch. "Nice to meet you, man."

"Yeah, same. So what's up, Emery, what's this about?"

She readjusts, sitting up so that one leg is beneath her on the couch. "Yeah, I'll make this good and short. So Torrey runs a bee farm down in LA city proper and because his grandfather is a nitwit and messed up some stuff, the property is being seized by the city."

"I see."

"Yeah," she says, continuing, "So, Torr wants to fight back. But we don't know what his options are."

"He owns the farm?"

"Right here," I say, hand raised. "Yes, the farm is mine. As in, my name's on the papers."

"His uncle willed it to him." I feel Emery's shoulder touch mine, and I know it's an intentional thing. This is Emery Grymchan being "comforting." She tries, guys. She does.

"Does he own the land the farm sits on or just the deed to the business and its assets?"

"Yep. I am still right here. And no, not the land, but yes to . . . all the other stuff, I think."

He leans back at his desk, the stress taking effect as he rubs the back of his neck. This is just an add-on, I know. Dude works four jobs, and Emery and I are a couple of pissy, green college freshman yanking on his shirttails.

"First, you gotta know what's yours and what isn't. Because if the land isn't yours, really the city can take it back at any time for almost any reason. What neighborhood exactly?"

"Echo Park," I say.

"Mm. A pretty hot gentrification spot right now."

I shrug. I mean, yeah, but do these things come in waves? I feel like the Hill's been getting snatched up spot-by-spot for my entire life, but it never really touches us—my neighborhood.

I guess I just really am that young.

"Yeah," he says. He grips the bridge of his nose, squints. "So here's what I can tell you. Find out what's yours legally. Once you've done that, and based on what you've told me, I'm going to assume it boils down to just the business and not the land it sits on, the only real pushback the city might recognize is a show of neighborhood support as well as proof that the city or—even better—the county benefits from the business's placement, not simply its existence."

"How the hell would I prove that?"

"Like, a petition or something?" Em says. I'd almost forgotten she was there. It's the quietest she's ever been, I think. Like in her life. Even asleep.

"Yeah, like, official neighborhood signatures—particularly ones of other businesses in the area."

I nod. "How beneficial would a social media push be?"

"Anything will help, but if you can get enough Internet media buzz going, you should have some solid footing to stand on."

"Alright. Yeah. Okay. Thanks, man. I appreciate the time."

"Anything for Emery Grymchan," he says. And he certainly isn't looking at me when he says it.

"Q, you are a god among men."

Dude shrugs like it's nothing, and I fight the urge to roll my eyes. He's practically falling asleep at the computer, has to work a whole-ass graveyard shift job, and has taken his limited (should-be-sleeping) time to talk to a couple of barely college freshmen. One of whom is a complete stranger to him.

"For you, it's nothing."

And Em waves and ends the conversation so quickly that I have to side-eye her. She definitely knows dude's got *feelinz*.

I give her a look to communicate that I know that she knows.

"Get out," she says. And that's the point at which I lose it and burst into hysterical fits of laughter. I do make my way out of her dorm though, only to hear her yell at my back as the door whispers shut, "Shut up. I will kill you, McKenzie!"

My legs feel stiff. I don't think it's from all the walking around I've done—my Health app says I climbed a total of three—COUNT 'EM, THREE WHOLE ENTIRE—flights of stairs today.

The stiffness, I think, is everything I want to walk away from. Talking to Ryan Q didn't help or add literally any value to my mission. It pretty much just told me I'm going to be tired for the rest of my life if I keep having to fight these battles. Fight for my right to exist and to exist on a level playing field. I mean, the apiary isn't my be all, end all. It's just another thing I have to fight for.

I don't have a choice.

Even if I did have a choice, would it matter? Would I stand

up and take care of things the way Uncle Miles would? The way he did so many times?

[oh shiiii bihhhhh flashback right here!!!!!]

I was sitting at the largest wooden table in America—conveniently located in Uncle Miles and Titi's very small apartment—when Uncle Miles walked in, a loose tie 'round his neck, lying against buttons on his shirt that had probably once been done up, but now spread the shirt collar apart.

He rolled his sleeves up as he walked by me at the table, cupped his hand around the side of my face for a moment—just a second—and then walked to Titi at the sink.

Usually, I'd look away. But this was some sort of quiet communication between them I hadn't ever seen elsewhere.

This was love.

Uncle Miles whispered something in her ear and she turned to him, smiled softly, and then walked out of the kitchen.

He took up her post at the sink, started washing the dinner dishes from a meal he hadn't even had a chance to eat yet.

Down the hall, the shower starts to run in the bathroom.

"I hear you got the elevator fixed in Mrs. Jericho's building," I said.

Uncle Miles did not look up from his task, but he did smile. Actually, it was more of a grin. "She's not mobile enough to get down the stairs. She was missing doctor's appointments." He said it like he had to justify this amazing and good and . . . just, not-his-job thing that he'd done.

"It's lit." I nodded my head up and down. Casual. That's me.

"Man, y'all out here with all these new catchphrases just ruining the English language."

I laughed, glancing down at my school-issued copy of Amal Unbound, *a smile perpetually painted on my face whenever he was around.*

"Talk to me about that homework you're working on, nephew."

And I did. I talked my way through all his dishwashing, at which point he sat down at the table with me, scooped up the mangy stray cat that sometimes hung around, and proceeded to talk to him about the cat food he'd promised to buy.

He was having a conversation with a cat, wherein, he promised—promised!—to have wet food for him tomorrow.

Even I felt reassured.

Typical Uncle Miles.

I need to go. To be there for my farm and to make sure nothing like this ever happens again. It wasn't something I'd have done by choice, but trusting Theo with even a fraction of responsibility—let alone the financial portion—for the farm was entirely moronic. I just thought that maybe, if Miles's name was attached to it, something other than self-preservation would matter to Theo.

My chest feels tight.

If you Google "Am I having a heart attack" and navigate to the series of YouTube clips they suggest, you'll be impossibly entertained. Go 'head. Do it. I'm not saying heart attacks are a laughing matter. I *am* saying I could definitely be the star of one of those stupendously dramatic heart attack reenactment videos. All I need is my 1:32 of YouTube fame, and I'm good.

Too bad what I'm feeling now isn't a heart attack. It's obligation. It's resolve.

It's right then and there, inside the quiet space of half an exhale, that I decide I'm going home.

I'm saying goodbye to this short second life of Torrey McKenzie.

15.

I take the stairs up Prominski Hall because the elevators lag for a ridiculous amount of time and there's always a herd of people idiotically waiting for them. Also, I feel like I need to prove something to my Health app. That's how they get you.

At the top, the heavy door swings inward just as I'm about to hit the push bar.

I nearly collide with a tall someone.

No, not nearly. I do. I completely and totally on accident throw my body at someone.

No, not someone. Gabriel.

He is more than a someone.

"Oh, shit!" he says on a laugh.

After his library exit I'm actually just super ready to hit my bed and hide from him for a couple (thousand) weeks. I'm a Taurus. Confrontation isn't my strong point. So whenever it becomes a thing I have to do, I internalize, needing time to gather my thoughts and figure out exactly what I need to say versus what I want to say. Also, and this is probably my downfall, I have this ridiculous tendency to map out what I think the other person will say. Obviously, this is super dumb. Because when they don't say what you think they will, problems arise. And it's your fault.

"What are you doing here?" It sounds a lot ruder than I expect it to.

He scratches the top of his head. Hair down and spiraling pretty much at its own whimsy, he pushes a rough hand into it and squeezes.

I am mesmerized. I am trash but also mesmerized.

"You."

"What?"

"I came here," he says, "To see you."

Pushing past him to move down the hall to my room, I riffle through my backpack for my dorm key. It's probably unlocked, to be honest. Desh doesn't understand personal safety or really any kind of general security. But I need something to do with my hands and as I reach the door, I grab the knob, key in hand, and it's actually locked. Desh isn't here then. And he did lock the door this time.

"Torrey," he says.

"I heard you. I just don't get why you're here after you bolted all fast at the library."

"Had to take care of something," he says without hesitation. Do you think he plans his conversations, too?

Gabriel steps forward and somehow we're both inside the room now, the door swinging softly shut with a final push by his hand.

His hand.

"So you bolted," I say.

"Well, when you say it like that!"

"I'm super confused by all of whatever this is. And I'm not saying it is something. But it just doesn't feel like it isn't. And I—" am not making any sense.

"I broke up with my girlfriend."

"Oh." What in the hell kind of answer?

"Yeah."

He doesn't hesitate. He presses into me and his lips meet mine, and I become a whisper of a boy.

Gabriel kisses me like I am his anchor to this reality, like he's looking for answers under my tongue, like I am the last taste of anything he'll ever have.

For me, time holds no relevance. He's shaking against me, but his lips are sure. His tongue in my mouth is a period, not a question mark. It goes on and on, like a poem.

Together, we are beautiful. There's no denying it.

Which is why I stop him as he begins to walk me back against the edge of my standard dorm-issue twin bed.

I stop him because this is too big to taint with questions. With rushed endings into even more expedited beginnings.

I want us to be a slow-stoked fire.

"Wait, wait," I say, pulling back. My lips are swollen. Gabriel Silva is a biter. That definitely was not the case in eighth grade.

He groans, pulling back. "You want me to wait more?"

"What do you mean 'more,' you weirdo. You're so impatient."

"You're too patient!"

"There really isn't such a thing as too patient."

Hands on hips, he paces the two-by-four box that is my dorm room. "You would say that."

"What do you mean you broke up with your girlfriend?"

He sits on Desh's perfectly made bed. For someone who swore he was never going to clean because his mother wasn't around to see it, Desh sure is pretty serious about having his bed made every morning.

He says, slowly, "I told her I could not be her boyfriend anymore."

"I understand what it means, Gabriel, Jesus Christ. I just need to know why you did it. I thought you guys were friends, even."

"We are," he says, coming closer. "That's why I did it."

I take a step back. "I'm not tracking."

"Torrey. Seeing you? Having you here? Having you in my life again—that was never going to work with Yuki. I did the adult thing. I was honest with her. I was already way too invested in what we had back then, and I'm even more invested now knowing that isn't over."

The silence crawling around inside me stretches for so long that Gabriel shakes his head, eyes going wide. "Unless . . . Unless it is over for you? I guess I should have asked first."

"It's not," I say. That's the honest truth. It's really not over for me. Slow burn, remember? "I just . . . there's so much going on right now. With my bees and back home with my family where I probably should be instead of this place."

"'This place'? Do you mean, like, school? College? Because I gotta say, Torr, it's a little messed up that you're here doing what is presumably the first step in trying to make it out of the hood, and you think this place is the one you shouldn't be in."

"I have to go back home, Gabriel. Shouldn't have even tried coming here. It was dumb as hell, I shouldn't have tried."

He shakes his head. "No. That's not true. And you are *already* here, Torr. There is nothing for you back there."

He's not getting it. He's not listening to me.

My chest feels white-hot, and there's this pressure in my throat that just . . . I have to get it out. "Everything," I say. "Everything I have ever known, ever been—ever will be—it's all back there."

He's in front of me so fast, grabbing a fistful of my shirt in one hand and then, just as abruptly, he lets go. "Listen to me when I say this. Are you listening to me?"

"Yeah."

"Torrey."

"Yes! I'm listening."

"Good. Hear me. You are more than that place, than those people, than this place and these people, too. You are the universe if ever I could see it in a single person. Do not let this thing become all of you. Some is okay. All is a waste of a very good thing. You're right to be here, bettering yourself. Giving yourself something good. You're right to do that. So, go. Go home for a couple days. It doesn't have to be all or nothing. Visit and get whatever it is you need. But then, after that, you come back. You come back here and plant your roots in this ground as deep as they'll go. Ficar comigo."

I surprise myself when I make my next move, pressing up as close as I can to him and my lips meet his again in a tangle, an inhale, a desperate exhale when it doesn't feel like enough. And I feel the joy of his smile on mine.

Gabriel pulls away first, pushing me back and going to stand in the farthest corner of the room. All I can do is look at him. He has to know what that kiss was. It was a warning. It was a message: This thing will consume us both, and I'm already shackled to something that's always been bigger than me. I don't know how to be any other way.

He does a series of ballet turns toward me, just enough to get him across the tiny room. He makes it seem bigger than it actually is. Although I suspect that's just Gabe. All movement and perfectly crafted lines in a difficult space.

"Pretty cool trick," I say, sitting down on my bed.

"It's not a trick. They're called pirouettes. Torrey, do you want to date?"

I look up at him, standing just above me. "I'm not following. How did we get here from making out to pirouettes to this line of questioning?"

"I mean, I'm just asking. Like, I just want to know. Do you want to date? Not even just me—although, I hope it's mostly me—but anyone. Do you want to date at all?"

I hesitate. I do. Obviously, I do. But I don't know how that can work if I'm trying to give everything I have to something else. Gabriel is all risk and wild decisions. But me? I am hesitation. I am Gabriel's antonym. The Taurus to his Pisces.

I hear Lisa's voice in my head. *You're going to kill yourself one day, trying to give away your entire self to the wrong thing.*

"Yeah," I say. And I . . . don't think I really realize it's just come out of my mouth. Definitely did not authorize that. But it's true. I want to date him. Slow burn. I want him.

"Yeah?" he says, crouched just in front of me now, hands on the ripped knees of my old-ass black jeans.

"Yeah. I want to date."

"Uhh . . . me? You maybe wanna date me?"

"I kind of definitely wanna date you."

That's all the indication he needs to rush me, pick me up. Throw me over his shoulder and shout about how he's going to lock me up and make me a "kept woman."

There are swears. There are shouts. There is laughter—mine, but also his. There are "Torrey Aloysius, I am going to kick your entire ass!" threats when I manage to flip the script and pin him down on my bed.

And there is a breathless moment in time where he and I don't have to try.

There's nothing else in the world like it.

*D*o you ever wake up and feel like your dream is still going?
I do.

Right now. Right now, I feel like I'm still dreaming. It's because I can still feel Gabriel's lips on mine. Can still feel the bite marks he's left on my skin. The feeling of yes that he's left in my room.

In case you thought shit was about to get romantic, I'm here to let you know—all that stuff I feel . . . Desh can, too. And he won't shut up about it.

"So how was the seeeeeeex?" he says from his flopped position on my bed. He didn't have to whisper the last two words, he just can't do anything without level-ten dramatics.

"Shut up," I say. Oh, sick burn, Torrey.

"Fine! You don't have to tell me about the sex, just talk to me about how this all went down. One moment you're all," and here—the way he takes up this super-weird impersonation voice, not okay—"oh, my bees! Whatever shall I do? Le sigh."

"Desharu, I swear to God and also Jesus."

"Then tell me what happened, bro. I would tell you!"

"I wouldn't ask!"

"I'd tell you anyway, c'mon, man."

And I actually do decide to tell him. Because I really do want to.

I exhale. "And then he put his shirt back on and left like literally a minute before you walked in."

He's on his back, no longer flopped now. "So, no sex then?"

"No. Jackass."

"Can't I be excited for your personal success?"

"No."

"Well, I am, and you can't stop me."

I hate him sometimes. But I also kind of don't know what my life here would be like without his flop-ass.

We're both quiet a moment, and I can't even guess at Desharu's reasoning. He doesn't exactly have a "resting state." This is probably new territory for him.

I decide to first flip the silence on its head. "I need to go home, Desh."

He sits up fast. "What? Why? You can't."

I stare at him.

He stares back. "Can you?"

"No," I say. "Not really. But I think I'm going to try to go for, like, maybe a weekend."

"Why?"

"It's not obvious?"

"If you say 'bees,' Torrey, I'll have to fight you."

I laugh, get up, and grab a gym bag out of my closet. It's hideous. Royal blue, given to us on the first day of orientation. Inside it, a treasure trove containing two number two pencils, a campus map, a very small plastic water bottle, and a magnet that says I DO SFSU. Which—issa no from me, dawg.

There's a smile on my face, which means I shouldn't turn around to look at Desh when I say, "Okay, then I won't say it."

A second later, I feel his pillow hit the back of my head, hear him mutter, "Dumbass."

My phone chimes and Desh is saved by the bell.

"What's up, Emery, everything okay?" I say, tossing some hopefully clean shirts in a bag.

"Yeah, fine fine. Did you see that flyer for gamers? There was a whole bunch of them over by the campus theatre. I need a partner-in-crime to go with me to check out the group."

"CAKE wasn't down? Seems like a thing you guys all might enjoy." STEM girls and all. Like, I'm sure gaming counts in that acronym somewhere, doesn't it?

"Torr, don't be ridiculous. You're totally my first choice here."

Oh, I'm sure. "Your lies only hurt me because they are so poorly crafted."

"Okay fine, I asked Kennedy but she's rushing a sorority and can't be bothered. But you were definitely my second choice."

"Be honest."

"Goddamnit, Torrey, okay! You were my last of like eight or nine possible choices but only because I know you don't really give a shit about gaming. At least I asked you before I asked Desh!"

She has a point. "When's it at?"

"Tonight. I think they normally do a weekly thing but because this is the first meeting, they do a special thing for incoming freshmen. Are you mad, though?"

"Em, I couldn't be mad at you if I tried."

She exhales. "Good. It'd suck if my ninth pick was out, too."

"You're such an asshole."

"I know. So you want to meet me?"

"Yes. But also, no. I can't."

"Ugh, Torrey, you put me through all that only to decline! What thing in your life is more important than me? Tell me so I can kill it."

Emery was definitely one of those weird-ass theatre kids in high school. "I'm about to catch a bus down to LA for a few days."

She is so quiet over the line that I have to take the phone away from my face twice to be sure the call hasn't dropped. It hasn't. And after a few more silent moments, I can kind of feel her seething.

"Torrey, this has to stop. It has to. You can't keep doing this."

I throw a crewneck into my backpack and zip it shut. "You don't understand."

"Oh, I do. I totally do. But you need to understand that you are here in body and not at all in mind or spirit. You hate it here but only because that stupid apiary won't let you enjoy it. All you do is talk about how this is temporary and the bees are taking precedence."

Again, not wrong. But that doesn't mean any of this is easy to hear. "I don't know what you want from me, Em. I'm just doing what I have to."

"Let me ask you this: at what point does it stop being a thing that you have to consider a priority? At what point do you get to put yourself first? Who gets to decide when your role in it is over?"

I don't know how to answer any of that. Because I don't ever think about it. I can't, because if I do, it'll tear me in two.

"I have to get going," I say.

She growls—a literal growl—and curses a ripe thing. "Okay, shit. Fine, wait. We'll take my car."

"Emery—"

"Nope. I'm coming with you. Meet you downstairs in twenty."

And she ends the call.

Which reminds me—I slide into iMessage and shoot Lisa a text. She needs to know I'm coming. She needs to know the plan.

"If the look on your face is any indication, I think I might be in love with Emery now," Desh says, camera in hand. He holds it up close to his face, snaps a quick photo of *my* face, and then brings it back down to glance at the result. He smiles.

I literally hate him.

"I can't believe I agreed to come with you to this shit city, with its satanic traffic and all its poorly crafted freeways and unreasonably large number of people wearing socks with sandals."

"You didn't 'agree to come,' because I didn't invite you. You invited yourself. You have only yourself to blame."

"Semantics," she says. "But, look. We're here to get signatures, right?"

I nod. "Yeah, basically. Just here to inform people what's going on and get them to sign the apiary's petition."

"'Kay, so, that being the case—you've obviously made the right decision having me here. People don't say no to me."

Yeah, because she won't let them.

Emery is probably the best option to play Robin to my Batman. And, I mean, I guess in a perfect world, it's probably Gabriel that would've come with me. But that was nowhere near an option. Here's why—bear with me:

1. I didn't even want Emery here to witness the way I

become someone entirely different when I'm here. Home. I wouldn't want Gabriel knowing that I lose pieces of myself. Make myself smaller so that the people here will feel more comfortable around me.

2. It would only take Theo, like, eight seconds to pop in and make some gross, homophobic comment.

3. Theo would not be the only person to make a comment like that.

4. Gabriel's mine right now. Inside my head, he's mine and only mine and it feels really solid. Untainted. I like that for us. I'm not trying to hide him or whatever this thing with us is, but it gives me space to contemplate and, eventually (I hope), understand what's been happening and what this means for us.

The lot's relatively empty, although the series of stores in this bunch of tiny markets are jammed together like Lisa's toes in her favorite pair of peep-toes.

You won't tell her I used her (and her toes) as a metaphor, will you?

The thing that only neighborhood locals know is that there is always a backlot for parking. It probably hasn't been repaved in, like, half a century at least.

Emily pulls into a spot in the corner, cursing as her left tires dip into a rough hole while her right tires skip up and over a sharp speed bump.

"I hate this city."

"You hate this parking lot, not the city," I say.

She says nothing.

We step out, clipboard in hand, just waiting for signatures. The air is thick and warm but not overwhelming. We're close enough here in LA city proper that we get a little of reprieve off the water from Santa Monica and Zuma.

None of the back entrances to the stores are marked. I think maybe at one point in time, they were. But now they're just so poorly maintained that you either gotta walk around the front to figure out which is which, or you walk into multiple stores before you finally find the right one. No store owner in this Los Angeles strip mall wants you running in and out their back door if you're as young as we are/not going to buy anything. Not even by accident.

We push into the rickety steel screen door and I turn back to Emery, saying, "Don't slam it but make sure it's all the way shut."

She looks at me like I'm crazy but does it anyway. Emery's from Monterey, which is its own kind of beach town, but not in the same way as any Los Angeles beach town.

Daddy Mojo's used to be a barbershop.

It still is—don't mistake what I'm saying—but it's also a "café" that serves both soul food and sushi. Sounds more sus than it actually is. Daddy Mojo's has the best gumbo I've ever had, and I'm not super well versed in sushi, but I'll fuck up some spicy tuna.

It turned into something altogether queer and unheard

of when, as neighboring businesses back in the seventies, the then-Ms. Xu, at the age of twenty-two, having just taken over running her family's restaurant, fell for the barber's son next door, Maurice Jones II.

So basically just boy meets girl, girl likes boy, boy and girl run their families' businesses and eventually marry before merging them into one soul-food-sushi-bar where you can get a fade that'd save even the ugliest dude from rejection, a mean-ass plate of greens, and a sake bomb (as long as it's after 5:00 p.m. and not on a Sunday because Mrs. Xu is a God-fearing woman and that's the Lord's day—her words, not mine).

Mrs. Xu lights up when she sees me and all but runs up to me in her same old tattered apron. "Mojo! Toto's here!" she yells in thickly accented English. Woman speaks four languages but has never managed to call me anything other than the name of the dog from *The Wizard of Oz*.

Mr. Jones grunts something loud enough that we can hear him from the back.

"Toto?" Emery says with a smile. I'm about to throw her in a headlock, too, right along with Desh.

"Shut up," I say to her. "Hi, Mrs. Xu."

"You need to be in school!" she says as she accepts a hug from me. My frame dwarfs hers. "You need a haircut, too. You'll go see Mo, his chair is always free for you. Who is this? Who is she?"

This woman is the equivalent of five red pandas and approximately thirty-eight questions in a trench coat.

"This is Emery, Mrs. Xu."

"You go to school together?"

I nod. "Yes, ma'am."

"I thought you were gay."

Emery dies of laughter, but Mrs. Xu nods, sagely, saying, "Oh. I see. She doesn't know you like the boys."

Aaaaaand who here knows the Heimlich maneuver? Emery is going to need some assistance, as she is choking on some very serious hysterics.

"We're only friends," Em says, sobering. "I live down the hall from Torrey. I also am well aware that he likes the boys. It is really, very nice to meet you."

"Sit down, I'll bring you a plate. Too skinny and nobody likes that, sit down."

Once she's in the kitchen, the sound of pots and pans and plates clanging (it's a wonder there are any dishes left in the kitchen that are intact enough to eat off of), Emery asks, "Was she talking to me or you about being too skinny?"

It's anyone's guess.

"C'mon. If we don't do as she says, there will be hell to pay."

Following in my footsteps toward the well-loved cracked booth in front, Emery whispers, "She's like three feet tall, though."

I laugh. "Ever had crabcake cornbread?"

And it's not that much later that we've had exactly that delivered to the table and have wolfed it down, when Emery groans and drinks the last of her green tea. "You'll have to roll me out of here."

"You'd be making Mrs. Xu a very happy woman. Come on, let's go see Mr. Jones."

"He's not going to try to feed us, too, is he?" she says, just as we pass the threshold of the restaurant's side door, out into the barbershop's back entrance.

As soon as we step inside, the entire shop choruses, "Ayyyyy!" Hands all up in the air.

It's the standard welcome when you've been away at school, locked up, or you've been having some kind of grow-my-shit-out crisis.

My fade is pretty fresh, but Mr. Jones gestures at his chair for me to sit and then walks away briefly to grab a seat for Emery to sit in, placing it right next to his station. The seat of honor for sure.

"Thank you," she says.

"Mm-hmm," he serves back. Mr. Jones is a man of few syllables and even fewer words. Translation for that one: Pleasure is all mine, Missy.

All Black girls under the age of thirty-five are "Missy" to Mr. Jones. Lisa's been pissed about it for a very long time now.

My thumbs drum the back of the clipboard as I point around the shop and spout off names of the men seated. Some waiting for cuts, some are just other barbers, the dudes who literally just sit here all day to hang out and clown one another, then finally, formally, Mr. Jones, the owner/the only man Mrs. Xu is nice to for longer than a few minutes at a time.

Robert, the barbershop assistant manager, calls to us from his station, "You get kicked out already, Torr? That ain't take long."

"No, I'm just here to tutor your dumbass as a form of charity for the hopeless."

The men sitting in the waiting chairs, folding sections of newspaper for a read, chuckle softly.

"Man, shut up and introduce me to your friend."

"She doesn't date down, Rob, but this is Emery."

She waves.

"She single?"

"Not for you," Emery says. "She also has ears and a mouth of her own."

That's it. She doesn't even realize she's won the entire crew at Daddy Mojo's over just like that.

The oldhead in the corner folds his newspaper down. "What brings you back around this way, T? Thought you were our success story. Thought you made it out the hood." That's Uncle Rudy. He's not really my uncle. I don't think he's anyone's uncle. But that's what we all call him, so I don't question it and neither should you.

Mr. Jones tips my chair back and takes some shaving cream and a blade to my sideburns and cleans up my beard, the blade pressed heavy to my skin just close enough that it could be called a kiss.

Mr. Jones, even as a longtime fan of brandy, has the surest hands in all of LA county.

"You heard about the apiary?" I call over to Uncle Rudy.

"Yeah, I heard about it. Same thing happened over on Ninth to, what's his name, the liquor store over there?"

I do my damnedest not to flinch at this. Still a blade sharper than Mrs. Xu's tongue on my face. "They seized Mr. Jimmy's store?" Jesus Christ.

"Yeah, Jimmy Wesley's whole thing down there," he says.

Another oldhead, fedora tipped at the only acceptable angle, chimes in, "Bought up that whole lot down there, too. Where all them apartments used to be. Too many people out here sleeping in them, I guess. Can't let poor folks have nothing."

If that ain't the truth.

Mr. Jones finishes me up, raises my chair, then spins me around and hands me a mirror. I look but not to inspect. Just to appreciate. I don't even have to wonder if he's gotten it right. That's just Mojo. Surest hands. Best eye. Largest heart.

I try to hand him some cash, but he grunts and turns to grab his probably-older-than-Methuselah broom to start sweeping up.

Emery stands, presses a kiss to Mr. Jones's cheek, which he accepts with a grunt and the smallest smile. You'd really have to be looking for it to know it was there.

"We're petitioning," I say. "What's happening out here isn't okay. White people are literally targeting and buying up our neighborhood so they can give it a face-lift and then price it at three times what any of us can afford."

"How is a petition supposed to help?" Uncle Rudy says, a laugh buried deep in his gut. "That's just some paper, right?"

I knew when I came here with this plan in mind that I would have to explain this in ways that made sense to them. "I talked to a lawyer friend. He says—"

Someone in the corner, some youngish dude covered top to bottom in FUBU gear, calls, "Man, I ain't trying to hear about that gay shit, so if that's what's about to happen, I'm cool on all that."

No one else speaks up. Some laugh. A few of the barbers glance up for literally a second and then keep it pushing with their clippers, wrist jumping up the crown of a head.

I push on. What else can I do? This isn't the place to confront homophobia. This is a barbershop full of cisgender heterosexual Black men who aren't here for that shit.

"He says if there are enough signatures, enough shows of support from local businesses, that it might force the city to hear me out on an appeal. It could even halt a lot of what's coming for any other businesses out here about to be torn down."

That same dude in the corner mutters, "Good luck with that. Soft-ass."

Mojo snatches up my clipboard, signs his name and contact info, then growls, "Both of y'all knuckleheads, get up on out my shop."

I'm pissed enough that I don't even bother going back the

way we came. I just push my way out the front door, its bell screaming above me. We're gonna have to walk all the way around the fucking block to get back to Emery's car.

Oh, goddamnit. Emery. I turn around to go back for her but she's right behind me. We stop and just stare at each other for a second. The look on her face . . . it's familiar, but also it's a little unwelcome. I hate getting that look from people.

You know the one—brows pushed together, lips pulled in as close to the teeth as they'll go, shaping some kind of smile-frown that says, *I'm sorry*. But for what? What should Emery be sorry for?

I curse and she pulls me into a hug, but it's a quick one. I think she knows that's all I'll accept right now.

"Which way back to the car?"

I point and we start down the hill, the heavy LA sun licking up the back of our necks as we trek along.

Back in the car, Emery blasts the AC and then exhales as she backs out.

There's a headache creeping right up under my left eye.

"Creep." Left Eye. Hilarious.

We spend most of the rest of the day hitting up the major businesses in the neighborhood.

Mr. Mark's discount tire shop, Tires By Mark—he is very original that one—Ms. Ollie's bakery, Ms. Sima's, the lady who does threading and waxing just above the old check-cashing spot me and Moms used to always hit up.

Not all of them sign. Some lecture me about messing with stuff I have no business trying to touch. Others say they can't risk getting involved in anything that'll bring the government or the cops to their door. A few more joke that if the money's right, they're taking it.

For niggas in this part of the hood, any amount of money is "right."

We're speeding down the hill, into the neighborhood when Emery speaks again. "Are we gonna go see your bees?"

I shake my head. "Nah, it's getting dark. Nothing much to see when the sun's down."

"Okay, so . . . to Theo's?"

I hate this, I hate this, I hate this. "Yeah. To Theo's. Take a left here and cut through the alley."

Christ, this neighborhood. I really hate this.

alking up the steps to my house feels like a lie. The porch no longer sings memories or nostalgia. Instead it reminds me that I spent too many triple-digit afternoons sitting on the warm, weather-roughened surface alone all because Theo wouldn't let me inside. It always happened after some supposedly effeminate thing I'd said or done. That was always the punishment.

Sit on the steps, legs crossed over the knee, and no talking. He'd say, "That's the way a bitch should sit." A display, not a noisemaker.

This house doesn't feel like a home anymore. And as I think

back to being a bony thirteen-year-old kid, I realize it never did.

Auntie Lisa's in my face and in my arms, all wrapped around me, fussing the second I twist the knob and cross the threshold.

And then she hugs Emery, too, despite not having met before. But that's Lis.

"Hi, Lisa," I say. "You owe me twenty dollars."

"Negro, shut up and come inside," she says, holding onto me like I'll leave her and float away forever if she doesn't.

"Twenty dollars?" Emery says.

"She bet me she wouldn't cry."

As she walks by, Lisa lands a swift swat to the back of my head. My shoulders kick up to my ears.

"Y'all ate?"

"We went to Daddy Mojo's."

Emery slips onto one of the bar stools at the counter. As a kid, I always remember them being a set of four. They're still four now, but two of them don't match, one of which isn't even really the right height.

"How'd it go over with Mo n' 'em? They sign your petition?" Lisa shakes ice from inside a large 7-Eleven cup into her mouth and chews louder than armageddon.

Also, sidebar: Lisa's the best at codeswitching, I love it. Okay. Carry on.

"Mr. Jones signed, but everyone else over there was skeptical."

Lisa nods. She knew it'd be an uphill battle. That's what the nod says to me. "You'll have a smoother time with the others."

"Ms. Nettie's gonna be a cake walk, she loves m—"

Lisa shakes her head. "They shut her down, T baby, the flower shop ain't up there no more."

My chest tries to twist its way off my body. "They closed it?"

"Took it. Closed it. Sold it. And then chopped it down."

Emery and I glance at each other.

"What's gonna happen with the land then?"

Lisa exhales. "Your guess, my guess, same difference."

The feeling that hits me isn't shock so much as . . . I don't know, remorse, I think. Moms and I used to walk by there a lot. Ms. Nettie was always real nice to us. To Moms. That was important to me. Because not many people in the neighborhood were willing to do things like bring us half a pot of leftover spaghetti or give Moms a few days of work when cash was tight. Or when cash was just straight-up nonexistent.

"Torr," Lisa begins. And I know she's about to say something I won't like. "Maybe we need to just figure out how to get through this shit, instead of trying to get from up under it."

"Okay, Lis. You tell that to Miles."

Emery stands. "I'm gonna go call Kennedy."

Aunt Lisa gets up, walks to the sink, and leans against it as though she can push the entire thing, counter and all, into the street just beyond the window. "I just want more than the hood for you, Torrey, and Miles would have wanted that, too. Even above the apiary."

159

I feel a river of hot resistance try to grab me and drag me under.

"I can't," I say on a rasp. A wheeze. A whisper that is trying hard to be something more like a rush of tears. Crying around Lisa isn't usually an issue. But after today, at the barbershop, I don't feel like crying is a thing I'm allowed. What kind of man . . .

"You can. Miles would not want—"

"It's not about Miles; it's about me and how much I owe him for having to raise some gutter kid who ain't even his!"

It's quiet a moment. Emery comes back in.

Probably intentionally. Em is a mediator. She's like the Spider-Man of shutting down arguments.

Her Emery Senses were probably tingling.

"We're cool," she says. This tactic always works for her because she fucking says it does.

So Lisa and I disengage from whatever knock-down-drag-out was about to happen.

"I love you," Lisa says. And I feel like shit. She continues, "And I love the apiary. But if there's an ultimatum, it's you, Torr. Every time. I hope you know that. You matter, too."

I don't say anything. I can't. I'm a breath away from breaking.

Theo walks in, and my breaking point morphs and becomes something entirely different.

I knew he was home. He's always home. But I'd held on to something resembling hope that I wouldn't have to see him. Usually he keeps his distance, even when I lived here twenty-four hours a day. Probably thinks gay is contagious.

Lisa ignores him as he walks in. She used to try and engage him, but that effort quickly died. "Pray on it, Torr. Honestly. I know we joke about this, but just give it to God, okay?"

As he drops his coffee mug into the sink, Theo says, "God don't deal with y'all little sweet boys. Ain't no reason to go His way because He don't swing yours."

And then he's gone, up the stairs to his cave of a bedroom, where he will not exit until he realizes he is a human male and has to eat eventually.

Lisa shakes her head. "I'm so sorry, Torrey. You know he just—"

"Do not make excuses for him, Lisa, I swear to God. He not *just* anything, unless you were going to say he's a homophobic shitbag of a human."

I glance over at Emery, who's standing completely still with her hand over her mouth. She's in shock at what just happened. I sometimes forget that's not normal behavior from someone who is your grandfather.

"Okay," Lisa says. Now she will try to de-escalate the situation. "Okay. Let's just sit down and figure out what spots we can hit up for signatures."

I exhale and gesture for Em to come sit next to me on the couch. I feel like I should have protected her from seeing that just now.

She sits. And though there's a ton of room on the couch, she all but sits on my lap.

She laces our fingers and squeezes twice. I squeeze twice back and plan out the route we'll take to keep my bees safe, too.

*T*he rec center is where I spent most of my time before everything with Moms went down. It's where I spent most of my time afterward, too.

Now, getting signatures from the people here just seems like a no-brainer.

They know me. They understand me. I've been refereeing for the local rec center's youth sports programs for about three years now. I fell into it after Lisa and Uncle Miles found me ditching school at the beginning of sophomore year and forced me to do this as a punishment.

Aunt Lisa disciplines like a Black mom, so when she sets

restrictions, you take that as bond.

I'd ref two games a week on Saturday mornings.

Since the kids are all ages eleven and under, the games can get pretty emotional, and there's clearly some latent skill, like this one short Black kid, Marc Antony—Mr. "Call me 'MA.'"

Just before the buzzer goes off to end the game, he launches the ball toward the basket in an arc that should have been impossible for that shrimp of a child.

Two kids more than twice his size make a leap intended to distract his shot. MA's all game, all focus, and I keep an eye on his hands to gauge the timing of it.

Still, a moment after the ball leaves his hands, the buzzer sounds, and the ball sinks into the net like it was running home.

MA's team loses the game, but their side of the sweaty gym still goes wild. Moms and coaches and attempting-to-be-supportive siblings everywhere cheer.

That's half of why I used do this thing every weekend, three years long.

I forgot how much I miss it.

"Hey," a voice says from behind me.

My cousin Rhyan, all of five-foot nothing. She grabs me in what she thinks is a firm grip by the arm.

"Wow," I say. "I thought a fly was running repeatedly into me or something."

She rolls her eyes. "I wish that was funny, but it didn't even make sense."

That's my cue to wrap my arm around her very-low-to-the-ground shoulders.

"Oh, my God," I croon. "Did you have a growth spurt, RhyRhy?"

"Oh, my God," she mimics. "Did you consider shaving your patchy beard, Tor-Tor?" She wiggles from underneath my arm toward her sister, who is the only girl on the winning basketball team.

"Good game," Emery says to Parris.

Parris is a nine-year-old of few words. She holds up her hand for a high five and says nothing as she reaches to her side and slides her slender arm around my waist with a murmured, "Hi, Uncle Torrey."

We're cousins but don't ask me to clarify the way Black familial relationships work.

"Good game, shorty mac."

She rolls her eyes. I know she learned that mess from Rhyan, who is almost twice her age. And then she walks off toward their mom. My aunt. A fierce-ass woman I gained by way of the world's most toxic marriage. We were all glad when my uncle Phoenix left them and never came back. We'd have found a way to trade Aunt Aimah for my verbally abusive, short-tempered shitbox of a human, Uncle Phoenix.

They say there's one in every family, but mine had Phoenix and Theo, so I often wonder what the rest of us did to deserve that.

"Who's your friend?" Rhyan says.

I turn and completely forget that Emery has been right there with me this entire time. Hard not to get lost in this place. In this town, in this city.

"Rhyan, this is Emery. She goes to SFSU with me and has agreed to turn me straight. Emery, this is my cousin Rhyan, we found her behind a Wendy's and decided to keep her."

Both of them hit me. Multiple times. More times than I deserve, IMO. But then they're shaking hands.

"How's it going with your Gore stuff, Rhy?" I say.

"You really don't want to know that. I know you're just asking because you left and you're feeling like you have to."

"I'm not. I honestly want to know—"

She laughs. "No, you don't, Torrey. It's okay. You can't even call it what it is. Gore Whoring. I am a Gore Whore. It's what I do. I like it, it's fine, and I'm not ashamed of that at all."

Nor should she be. It's just weird for me as her older cousin. Even if it's just older by not that much. I don't even really know what it is. As far as I can tell it's just a lot of cosplay that involves fake skin, colored contacts, and scantily clad photo shoots and Twitch streams.

It's a whole community, according to Rhyan. Those are her people, which is interesting since she doesn't really have any, like, real-life friends that I know of.

"Fine, how's the Gore Whore stuff going?"

Yep, I get another eye roll. "It's going, Torr. What do you need?"

Nothing much, I think. Just need to know that there's something in this city worth coming back for that isn't about the bees.

I wipe away whatever expression I know is on my face and paste a Band-Aid over it in the shape of a smile. After Emery and I make several circuits around the rec center, clipboard and a little hope in hand, I make my way back to the basketball courts to hug Rhyan, Auntie Aimah, and Parris for a few good, long heartbeats.

Most people don't know that there are more than twenty thousand species of bees, only four of which are honey bees. And why should they? I mean, did you know that? It's okay if not. It's a useless fact, for the most part.

Unless you're me.

The vast majority of our hives make somewhere around four hundred pounds of honey each.

I mean, we're not making bees our indentured servants or anything, but the stuff we harvest and jar is some of the best honey in the greater LA County.

And selling the honey isn't our only goal. Sure, we like being able to provide that here at Miles To Go. But we also like educating people—kids—about bees. About honey. About the similarities between a beehive and this neighborhood and how they're both equally feared and revered.

Which brings me to this: Emery's utter speechlessness at the greatness of Miles To Go. Emery stayed the night at the house, where she took up half my bed and used all the hot water in the shower.

Those were our only two points of conversation. She tries multiple times to talk to me about what happened with Theo but I shut her down abruptly and harshly.

It's only the next morning that we start speaking on something like normal terms, pop-up waffles and cups of tar-black coffee in hand.

"This place is literally a diamond in the rough, Torr. Starting to get what you see in this beekeeping stuff."

Sidebar: I love how "literally" isn't even a *literal* term anymore.

We push through the side gate, which doubles as the entrance to the storage shed and enter the garden. The grounds of the apiary itself aren't incredibly huge. But what's there is covered in wildflowers and lavender. The wildflowers are pretty easy to maintain in the LA heat, the lavender takes a little more effort. My favorite recent add is the dome-shaped glass flower box. It's a nice touch, with its seafoam-colored glass. And with the way the metal bars overlay the top, it looks like honeycomb. It's excellent for the keeping of our largest hive. Aside from that one, affectionately nicknamed Papi Chulo, there are a dozen other moderately sized bee boxes made of cypress wood (not pine wood, though many people will try to tell you it's the better option—they don't know anything, don't listen to them).

Considering our location, right in the hood's congested

heart, the grounds are fairly quiet. As quiet as Los Angeles ever gets, I'd say.

Emery is, naturally, a little skittish as we walk through to the front of the apiary where the shed is. People fear bees because one jackass with an allergy dicked around and got stung, then told us we should shun them.

"Torrey," she says, wary.

I grab her hand. "Don't trip. I got you."

"What if they sting me and I'm allergic and I swell up like a Macy's Thanksgiving Day Parade balloon and die?"

"We're prepared for that particular scenario, but I'm pretty sure you'll be fine." I could bore you with the specifics and statistics about people who are deathly allergic to bee stings, but I won't.

Emery still seems skittish as we walk past and through the slow-blooming flowers along the grounds, so I pause.

Realistically, bees, especially honeybees, are incredibly fucking cute. With their round, fuzzy little bodies that seem way too heavy to be carried on their thin, gossamer gold wings. I've had a lot of time to think about the makeup of bees. Sue me.

"You wanna harvest some honey?" I ask.

"Um, yes?"

"It's fun, I promise."

We head inside the storage shed. It should really be way more organized than it is, but I'm the one who usually handles that and with me gone . . . well. There's a laundry list of things that fall apart when I'm not around.

Lisa's good at running the large-scale things but organized, she is not. She says it's "the mark of a good scientist." I say it's bullshit.

Pushing that as far out of mind as possible, I pull two bee-keeping suits from a small closet, just inside the shed. It takes longer than usual to get all kitted up into them because I help Emery, step by step, with getting hers on first.

"Take your shoes off and put on these," I say. She's wearing these tiny flats with bows on the back, and the top of her foot is all kinds of exposed, and that's just no good.

She takes the rainboots that Lisa usually wears and puts them on slowly, followed by a pair of thick elbow-length gloves and then, finally, the "helmet" of the suit. "Will you take a picture of me?" She laughs. "I wanna post it on Insta."

Ridiculous. But of course I do it. Because if you harvest honey for the first time, and you don't post it on Insta, did it really even happen?

She posts it, one glove off, and captions it accordingly.

@EmeryBoard: BEElieve it or not, I'm doin' this!

I stare at her flatly. "That caption just gave me tuberculosis."

"Judgy! Shut up and make me some honey."

Wheelbarrow, smoker, a bit of paper and dried lavender to go inside it, and a gentle brush and a hive tool to help me crack the hive open. Bees are actually pretty brilliant. They like to seal the hives shut nice and tight to protect the honey inside. Smart, right?

Emery, hyped up on the idea of wearing the harvesting suit but not so much on the actual harvesting itself, gets a little uneasy again.

I take her hand. "The smoker will make it so that the bees are relaxed enough not to bug you much. They can't reach you inside your suit."

"Yeah. 'Kay. Okay."

"You alright?"

She nods.

"We can stop."

"No, no, no. I already posted the picture. We're doing it."

"Alright."

I hand her the smoker. "Squeeze this."

She pumps it a few times, and smoke bellows out of it, dry and sweet, paper and lavender.

While she does this, I remove the closure on top of the hive and then use the hive tool to peel the second closure off.

She gasps. There's nothing like watching someone look inside an active hive for the first time.

Inside the boxed hives are the frames where the honey is stored.

I pull one out, and it's dripping with honey.

"Oh, my God! Look at it!" Emery says and I have to laugh.

"Grab that soft brush," I say. And she does. "Okay, so now, *gently* brush the bees away from the frame. Gently."

A kid in a candy shop. Like walking through a chocolate factory and getting to manifest the sweetest thing on Earth, all on your own. That's its own sort of magic.

"How often do you do this?" Emery says.

"Harvest?"

She nods and continues to brush the stray bees off either side of the frame. "Yeah."

"There's really no set time. My uncle Miles used to say that beekeeping isn't selfish. You're only supposed to take the *excess* honey and nothing more. Bees still need it to survive, and they can't collect nectar for honey making year round. So, they need reserves for the off months."

"Makes sense. I kinda like that."

We manage to extract three frames full of ready-to-harvest honey and then wheel them back to the shed after recapping the hives with their crown boards.

Inside, mostly free of our heavy suits, I hand Emery what looks like—and, honestly, kind of is—a machete.

"Watch," I say, and then I begin to scrape off the top layer of wax covering one side of the frame. Emery goes to work on hers.

What's funny, but not at all surprising, is that she's better at this than I am. She was even humming to the bees as she brushed them away from their cells on the frame. My movements are clumsy and too fast and just messy. The product of having done this for too many months of my life. Hers are quick, but also clean and smooth. Looks like art, the wax coming off the top of the cells in the most satisfying of ways. A stark contrast to our next step.

I grab three of the frames in one arm and Em's hand on my other side, leading her to the extractor—this oversize metal barrel.

"What's this for?" she says, leaning over it to look inside. There are remnants of honey and wax from other extractions.

"You'll see." I hold the stacked frames out toward her. "Slide these in there one by one. Yeah, just along the sides. Mm-hmm, like that."

"Like this?"

"Yep. Here." I instruct her to grip the handle on the barrel as tight as she can. And then she begins to crank, spinning the handle clumsily, but with determination that soon turns into finesse. She's so good at everything.

Sometimes, when people show promise regarding beekeeping or honey harvesting, I instinctively know and understand that they're just naturally good at everything. Beekeeping isn't difficult, but it isn't easy either. Takes time and understanding and patience. A thing most people don't come equipped with.

But Emery? My girl's a natural. And I have this weird infusion of pride swimming through my veins, watching her. To be the person who shows her this. Who gets to experience her experiencing it—that feels almost as amazing as doing it all myself.

It's the thing that gives me the most joy in this place. The teaching. The watching. The way others can find so much joy in this very small, almost unknowable skill.

Because when I tell people that I *keep bees,* that I own a farm for beekeeping—they do a double take. They see a six-foot dark-skinned Black kid from east LA, and they see one thing.

I'll leave that *one thing* to your imagination. Which is funny, because that's my reality.

As Emery spins the handle, the frames inside start to whir in circles around the extractor.

"Faster," I say. "The faster you go, the easier it is for the honey to drip into the bottom of the barrel. You'll see less wax in the barrel when it's all bled out."

She's breaking a sweat now, but the light in her eyes is the same color as the honey, and this is the picture of someone enjoying themselves. She'll be sore in the morning. All through the arms and shoulders; probably her back, too.

"Want me to take over?" I shout over the noise of the extractor.

She shakes her head but doesn't look up at me. She's so focused on the honey, the slow drip dancing its way out of the cells.

"You'd think you're trying to get this thing to fly."

She stops spinning, the crank still moving without her, and stares up at me, deadpan.

I grab the lever, attempting to conceal my chuckle at the look on her face.

"Why're you stopping it?" she says, breathing heavily.

"Look," I say and pull out one of the frames. The honey's completely escaped from the cells, so I open the spigot at the bottom where honey starts to drip into the bucket we place below to catch it and funnel out the larger bits of wax. "We gotta give it time. We'll go swap out our suits for clothes, and then wash the stickiness off. When we come back, most of that will have separated."

I laugh as we're walking out of the shed; Emery can't seem to look away. She keeps glancing back at the extractor and the honey dripping out of it, like she's leaving her child behind or something.

"Don't you laugh at me, Torrey McKenzie, this has been a labor of *love*."

I throw my arm around her shoulders. I know the feeling like I know breathing.

Changed now, and back in only our street clothes, Emery follows me out of the office.

"Torrence!" Lisa calls. I love the woman but goddamn, she's loud. Although I don't complain or tease her about it because she really is doing me such a solid with the farm. It's really Black women saving me all the time, and I don't even know what it says about me that I gravitate toward that kind of aid.

Or the fact that they save me, and I accept it, but I only occasionally wonder who's saving them.

"God, I am so glad to have you back on farm grounds, Torr. You've no idea."

"Emery is like ninety percent of the reason I made it in one piece."

Em shrugs, says, "So this is cool as heck. How even do you guys manage to hold something like this down?"

Lisa runs her hands up into her hair. "By the skin of our teeth lately, it seems."

On an exhale, I say, "I come from a long line of 'How dare you fix your mouth to ask me for blah blah blah . . . ?'"

"Yeah, and 'Give it to Jesus, baby. Just give it to Jesus—there ain't nothing He, capital H, won't do for you,'" Lisa says.

"So what you're saying is, you go it alone?" Emery says. She looks sad. Emery comes from a home where both of her parents are still married. Emery has never had to figure out where her next meal was coming from, what she'd have to pay to get it, or worry about whether the lights would be shut off when she got home from school.

That's not necessarily a problem. But . . . it's different than what I know. My phone, nestled in my back pocket, buzzes. It's a call from Gabriel. I hit decline so fast, I just know both the girls saw it. It buzzes again, and Lisa's eyebrow creeps up her forehead.

Judgy.

I think about my mother and our kitchen in Theo's house with the two orange lights that flickered on and off and on and off, and I wonder if they were a metaphor for the bad habit of love I learned—when you get accustomed to a dimly lit love, a dimly lit room, you forget about what it's like to be kissed by the sun, to be loved so fully. It's only when you walk away, when you sell the house, when the sun comes up in the morning, that you realize you deserve the light. You deserve it all. This kiss and this radiance. I wish I could have held myself a long time ago, but now here I am, running in the opposite direction of the light every time my phone sings.

I mean, the last thing Moms ever gave me was silence and my heart torn open like a pomegranate. She'd made me promises about sobriety I knew she wouldn't keep. I believed her anyway, because that's what you do.

Conversation fades back in. ". . . And I really think you'd get along with some of them if you ever decided to come up and visit with us for a weekend or something," Em is saying. "Right, Torrey?"

"Huh? Oh! What? Yeah. I mean, yeah, I definitely think you should."

Lisa laughs. "We'll see. I might be too old to try and keep pace with y'all."

"Oh, my God. You are *not* old!" Emery is *really* laying it on.

And Aunt Lisa knows, too. "Torrey, if you got this, baby, I'll catch up with you two at the house." But Emery's already wandered off.

She's walking through the section of the farm where we've recently started to grow sunflowers. The lavender and wildflowers are great, but the sunflowers remind me of LA. Better for nothing other than looking at how big, demanding, and gorgeous they are.

I laugh quietly as Emery bends to dramatically press her *entire* face into one of the shorter sunflowers, smiling this huge I'm-an-American-Girl smile into it as though this single, horrible-smelling sunflower holds the secret to finding her next relationship. She does a little twirl, and *that's* when I fucking lose it.

"Ready to go jar up your honey?" I can barely get the sentence out, I'm laughing so hard.

She turns around sharply. "How long have you been standing there watching me—"

"Pretending to be in a Taylor Swift music video? Not too long."

Her arm around my shoulders now, she says, "Shut up. I was going for Kelly Clarkson."

"Nailed it."

"If you say so."

"I *do* say so. Now, let's go get you some honey, honey."

Emery groans. "I was waiting for you to make that shit joke, and you folded *much* sooner than I thought you would."

"Shut up, I've seen your Instagram captions."

Back inside the shed, I pull out three large jars for filling. One for Emery, one for Lisa who likes to drop a little on a petri dish and look at it under a microscope, and one for Gabe.

I'm holding the bucket over the last of the three jars, watching honey spool into itself like a thick ribbon, when Emery says, "I can see why you love this. See why you do what you do. I can only imagine having spent most of my life surrounded by bees and honey and this atmosphere and this process. I'd probably be tethered, too."

I don't say anything. She's right. It's bees I'm tethered to. Bees and honey and preservation of a good thing in a quickly deteriorating space.

Right?

Or, okay. Yeah.

That, and guilt. I guess.

If I'm being honest.

Guilt c/o Uncle Miles.

Suits tucked away, selfies taken, and jars of honey in hand, Emery and I leave Miles To Go.

The real work starts here.

19.

'm up at the ass-crack of dawn, shooting off an email to another somewhat local apiary—the Addie Rose Apiary— just outside San Francisco county. They've always been a well of support to us at Miles To Go.

We spend the better part of the day, as well as the worse part of it, driving around for signatures. Half of downtown Los Angeles is tourist attractions like Chinatown, and the other half is traffic. But after living here, after knowing the hood better than I know myself or anything else, Emery and I make our way around the quieter streets. We drive around the neighborhoods and watch kids half our age shoot dice, some adults twice our age join in. We drive through La Cienega and back through 54th, too. As we approach each storefront, we lower the music out of respect and self-preservation.

Some streets out here are loud and exuberant. Expressions of who we've been as Black folk and who we damn near killed ourselves to be. Those are the neighborhoods that have not a damn thing left to lose. Those are what the mainstream media calls "the ghettos."

Those are the streets I was made on.

But this area, just up and east a few blocks, is quieter, muted in a desperate attempt to blend in.

The formula goes something like this:

Black folks + Quiet, law-abiding residents = No police interference.

Although, in reality, it really looks more like:

Black folks + Any volume, activity, or breath exhaled = Police and a bullet.

We spend six hours driving around the neighborhood, only two of which did we spend sitting in traffic (this is a success, I'm telling you), before heading back to Theo's. We set up shop upstairs in my old room and start making phone calls (Emery's idea) to some of our local honey buyers and suppliers, as well as a few of the LAUSD elementary schools that arrange annual tours of the apiary for their students.

The goal, according to Ryan Q, is that we need to make them see how valuable we are. How much the neighborhood and its residents depend on us.

Lisa watches from a distance as we call, walking slowly down the hallway, popping in to make sure we're "just doing okay." She wants to help. It's who Lisa is. But I can tell that she's also a little torn between helping and washing her hands of all things bees, as not to encourage me.

Little does she know, I don't need any encouraging.

Emery scoops up her towel and toothbrush, catching Lisa loitering in the hallway under the guise of folding sheets in the linen closet.

"Shower," Em says and I nod.

It's Lisa's cue to come sit with me.

She puts a hand on my arm. "I'm so happy you're here. I hate that you are. That you have to be. The circumstances are awful. But I'm a little bit lost without you, T." She smiles sadly.

I don't know what to say, and I think Aunt Lisa sees that, so she opts for a subject change. Which. I mean. *Thank God.*

"Oh, my God," Lisa says, "Did I tell you about the guy that came by here a few days ago?"

"Guy?" The back of my neck itches. "What guy?"

"Some skeeeeezy white-collar jockstrap wannabe type. The oily skeezy noodledick bro-dude type. He comes by, tries to finesse my name and some info about the farm and Miles and you and Theo."

Shit.

"Says he wants to buy the farm if I make it easy on him. Had all these lush promises in his mouth, talking butter."

(Translation for the whites: *Talking Butter, gerund phrase; to smooth talk your conversation partner, often includes promises of rewards, gifts, or grandeur. Or weed.*)

She goes on: "Says some shit about setting up Miles's widow real nice in the Hollywood Hills, getting me out of here."

I don't like this. "What'd he look like? White, money, greasy forehead, oil-spill black hair?"

"Mm. You know him?"

"Of him," I correct.

"Torrey, did this man approach you, too? *At school?*"

I nod. "Must've been right after you."

Nope. Not liking this at all.

"What'd he promise you? He say the same things to you?" There's so much urgency in her voice now, I can't handle it.

"More or less."

Her nose goes a little pink, and it looks like she's about to cry. "That is not okay. It's unsafe. And should be *illegal*. Did you tell him anything?"

"I didn't say anything." Nothing he wanted to hear, anyway.

I pause as an incoming call buzzes against my leg. It's Gabriel trying to FaceTime. I'm not great with random phone calls, let alone spontaneous FaceTime calls. But I should talk to him. If only so that there's some clarity and clean air somewhere in my life.

Lisa starts to walk out of the room, smiling. "It's okay. Go.

Take that. I'll be downstairs."

Later I will stop and feel bad about how quickly I swapped out Aunt Lisa's company for Gabriel's. Lisa, to whom I owe many, many gifts and favors.

To whom I will soon be—yes—*talking butter.*

I hold my breath to re-center myself. I'm holding my breath? Jesus. Well, there you have it—totally *not* just a thing girls do.

"Hi," I say.

Gabriel's face is a pixelated mess, but that's mostly because my reception always skips in and out when I'm upstairs, and Theo doesn't believe in the Internet.

"Hey, there," he says. And the way his eyeteeth always peek through that right-side-of-the-mouth smile he gets going on threatens to drop me. "How's home?"

I shrug and then remember that Gabriel knows me. Gabriel is my London, and London knew home wasn't home for me.

I tell him as much. "Yeah, it's not . . . that. Anymore."

"Mm. I get that. But the signatures, though? And your bees? That going okay?" Gabriel reclines on his bed so that he's all the way slumped down, turning over onto his side to prop his phone up right in front of him. It's like we're face-to-face and my racing thoughts that've tried to ride the top of my shoulders all day begin to slow.

I mimic his position. "Bees are good," I say. I smile at him because it feels good to, because even through the exhaustion, this part feels almost as good as a kiss from him would. "And, I guess, the signatures are adding up, but who knows if a court or judge or even a lawyer will find them valuable enough. How's academia without me?"

"Please, academia left the moment you did. Got a manicure and a new sew-in and went club hopping."

I have to sit up because otherwise I might swallow my tongue and my esophagus along with all the laughing that's happening. "Fair."

"Academia doesn't miss you, but I kinda do."

"Oh, *kinda*. I see."

"Do not flatter yourself, Torrey Aloysius. Yes, *kinda*."

I'm on a down pillow that I'm sure is having a lovely time of knife play with the back of my head. I pull it from behind me, chuck it at the floor.

At.

Not "to" or "on." At. Because fuck down pillows and comforters, amirite?

"You're the second person today who's used my first and middle names together. What have I done to warrant this?"

"I don't know but you deserve."

My eyes trace the fullness of his lips and the sensory tantrum of kissing him, pressing my every-damn-thing into his all-of-that comes coasting up on me like the shock of a defibrillator.

A lot of my life has been spent proving to myself that I am not prey. With Gabriel, every conversation begins with a game of who gets to play the part this time.

"You don't," he amends. Then, "Você é lindo."

Every hair on my body dances. When he speaks Portuguese, I just . . . Christ. "What did you just say to me?"

He laughs. "Nothing you didn't already know, I'm pretty sure."

"Foul play, my friend."

"All's fair, blah blah blah."

"You saying we're at war?" Or maybe the former?

"Something like that."

I'm a goner. I feel like someone's hooked up some sort of electric current straight onto my smooth criminals, and I have to change up my leg positioning to find any kind of relief.

"When do you get back?"

"Tonight. Pretty late though."

He picks at the cuticles of his nails. "Can I see you?"

Are you melting? I'm melting. "If you must."

"You're such a shithead."

"You like it."

"I do."

We're both quiet, just staring at each other, eyes reading braille against each other's faces.

"Do you think it's possible to fall in love with someone entirely, but only for a little while? Or are we just at that age where every small encounter with someone given to greatness seems like an amazingly large one?"

"I think," he says, and it takes him so long to continue that I want to smack myself for even asking. But then he does. And it's beautiful. "I think that love can be mighty, and so that's why people place limits on it. I think it's really that we can't believe something so big, so grand and perfect, can occur at literally any stage it wants to, for any length of time it damn well pleases. So, to answer your question, yes. I think it's very possible to fall in love with a person or thing for whatever length of time the moon allows. I think that love can be genuine and true from the moment you sustain that electric thing that lovers, apparently, get."

We make eye contact so unabashedly that I can feel my pulse touch his. It touches me back. And I know that sometimes love happens fast and whispers that it has every intention to stick around for the ride.

I drop my backpack literally at the threshold of my dorm room and collapse facedown on my bed. I'm exhausted, and it's just now hitting me. The physical heaviness of *I'm tired*.

My phone pings, and I open it—face still very much pressed into my mattress, I can multitask—to see an email from my academic advisor, who wants to speak to me about my classes, picking a major, and reminding me the Add/Drop deadline is coming up in a couple of days.

Lovely!

I thought I'd have time to figure this out but it's like they're trying to shove me off a cliff toward some legitimate and life-defining thing.

The truth is, I don't have any answer to that question, and I'm not the kind of person who's indecisive. I just like to have a basic understanding of the consequences to my actions. And if that means I gotta take my time, well, then: 🧍

And I understand the need to pick something if I'm going to stay here. It will dictate the rest of my class scheduling for the next however many years. It's not that I decided to go undecided because I'm not serious about college. I am. It was supposed to be my out.

Or, is. I meant it is supposed to be my out.

But obligation had other plans for me, and now the Add/ Drop is first—that decision that needs to be made before any major or minor or whatever. And I can say with all surety that obligation is going to hold me back from choosing a thing for me, the way it always fucking does.

He'd encourage you to save yourself before ever thinking about those bees.

Sitting up, I reach over into my side table drawer and pull out that stupid business card. Why the helllllllll did I even keep this thing? I should have set it on fire the second he tried to hand it to me.

Desh walks in. "Yo! You're back, I almost tripped over your old-ass backpack."

"My bad."

"No worries, I would never judge you because your backpack looks like it's from the 1970s. What's that? Calling up some nude ladies?"

"I am aggressively gay, Desh. I don't know how you would've come to this conclusion. Homosexual."

"Okay, but doesn't that business card look like the ones that're all over the strip in Vegas? The ones that are all black with silver or gold writing in some gaudy-ass font, advertising a strip club called GIRLZ GIRLZ GIRLZ for a fifty-cent entry fee or something?"

Yes. You can take a moment to question his sanity. That's totally fair, I'm doing the same. "I haven't ever been outside of California, so I'll trust you on this part."

"Never been outside this state? That's rank."

That's poverty.

"This guy approached me about the apiary. I think he might be able to help. He says he can."

"Call him," Desh says without a single moment of thought. I'm not someone who can just do anything. I think my decisions through. I have to.

But what's the harm in a phone call? I can totally hang up or back out at any time.

My phone's in my hand before I know it, and somehow with even more immediacy, it seems, he's on the line.

This is going to be a good thing. This is going to manifest the very beginning of my future. This call is going to set me up for success. It's going to prioritize *me*.

I exhale and then say, as soon as I hear him spout his name as a greeting, "I'm not saying I'm all in or totally willing to finesse any of this process for you. I just want to talk details."

There's a groaning sort of creak in the background and I picture him, reclining in his ergonomic office chair, smug and feline, immensely pleased with himself. Dickwad.

"I see," he says. "Well. I'm going to be straight with you, Timmy—"

"It's Torrey. And if you pretend to get my name, or my uncle's name, wrong one more time, I'm going to shove it up your ass."

He straight-up laughs at me. "Understood. Y'know, I like you, kid. I do. So here's what I've got for you. You're doing full-time school up there at your fancy SFSU, are you not?"

" . . . I am."

"Tuition's a bitch, isn't it?"

"I get financial aid. It's not too bad."

"We'll keep you covered. All four years, kid. Which means you'll essentially be pocketing the tuition you've already paid for this semester."

Is this a thing? I don't know what I'm doing here, and I'm in way over my head but I'm not entirely sure this is the legal way things are supposed to go.

He goes on. "And your mom? She's in that care center, right? Beautiful lady, by the way. We'll take care of her past-due payments. Sucks being in the red, I bet. We'll cover all future expenses for the year."

This feels like a threat. I'm young and maybe naive, but I'm not a fucking moron. He knows where my mom is and has even been to see her. I don't like it.

"We're here to help you, Torrey. We want what you want. We want to preserve your uncle's dream, to help it last. To make sure your bees are kept and kept well." He laughs at his own joke. I'll never understand the humor of mediocre white men.

I wonder who the "we" is that he keeps referencing. The one thing I don't know that I've ever had or will ever have in my life is financial security. And for an offer like this . . . I'm so tempted to let them be whoever the hell they want to be.

"How about this," he says. "How about I send you over some information? Let me take down your email, and we'll go from there. I'm traveling on some business the next few days. But I have a feeling I'll be around soon enough that you and I can talk shop."

Talk business. No. Everything about that exhausts me in strange ways. Maybe that's the work of exhaustion on top of exhaustion.

I'm tired. I'm beat down mentally, emotionally, which to be frank, feels much worse than any physical ass kicking I've ever gotten. And growing up where I did, running the streets the way I did—they happened often enough.

And there's really no getting around the fact that I'm doing this alone, for a neighborhood that thinks it's okay to physically assault me as I walk down to the corner laundromat. That thinks it funny to spray paint words and figures on the walls of my apiary. For a neighborhood that says they're just trying to make it to tomorrow, paycheck to paycheck, but doesn't want to do the work today.

Every night, I spend those hours dreaming about the thorns in my feet I've gathered in the midst of this neighborhood. I never dream about pushing back, about using my voice, about telling them how wrong they are about me.

But I want to.

I really, really want to.

"Just tell me what I have to do to make this happen."

"Excellent!" he answers. And it's almost too quickly. "Let's set a date and time to meet."

The sky is the color of a dusky bruise, a dirty plum, and a fat pool of scalding water all layered on top of one another.

I can only wax poetic about it because of the company I'm keeping at the moment. CAKE, Desh, some girl Desh has been "talking to" named Cheyanne, Gabe, and myself are seated in what the university calls the "Common Living Outdoor Patio."

It's not a patio, first of all. It's a bunch of benches and tables with some umbrellas over them located just behind the school's oldest building. But still, second, it's a space I'm pretty grateful for tonight, at what is possibly the darkest hour San Francisco ever sees as a city that chooses to sparkle instead of sleep.

My head's down on my folded arms as my friends speak around me, Gabriel's large palm stroking a path up and down my jean-clad thigh.

"Wake up, beautiful boy," he whispers.

I crack one eye open and then crack a smile, too. "Hello, don't tell me what to do."

He laughs and runs his lips across my temple. He does that, I've noticed. It's not a kiss, just a simple stroke and a steady inhale.

"What's got you so content?" he says.

"You," I say back.

"Oh, yeah?"

"Yeah."

Gabe shakes his head. "Nah. I'm not that special. What else—be honest!"

It's a really excellent feeling, to be able to do this with him. With anyone. "I think I might have fixed everything with the apiary. I think I can maybe let go of it now and not have to carry it by myself."

He shakes his head. He's not sure what I'm saying.

"There's a guy. An . . . investor? I guess?" I wet my lips and Gabe's eyes track it, so I do it again. "He says he'll take care of it. His company—I guess it's kind of what they do?"

On a slow nod, he says, "So . . . would you have to pay him something for this?"

"No, that's the thing! He's, uh, making it mutually beneficial. With no cost on my part."

He just stares at me but says nothing, and I really don't know how else to explain what happened, so I tell him, "Feel like I can breathe, Gabe. Feel like all the steel that's been soldered into my spine has been lifted out." This probably isn't the best way to talk about what's going on inside my head. I once watched a video in this article about a man who was having a steel rod *removed* from his leg. Know how they get it out? They take a hammer-like tool and basically swing it upward and into the protruding, exposed part of the rod until it's basically out.

They *beat it out of you.*

Still, I say, "I feel weightless, buoyant for the first time. And I've been so ready for this feeling for longer than I'm willing to admit, so ready to feel untethered to anything but you."

My favorite thing about kissing Gabriel has gotta be the fact that I never have to negotiate my way into it. I lean in, press my lips to his, use my tongue to trace the inside of his upper lip, and when he smiles into it, I hold that inside me. And it moves my heart into sweet, sweet ease, just like honey.

Some of CAKE's conversation floats back to me.

"Please, no private-parts talk at this table right now," Kennedy says. It's just like her. Private-parts talk.

"Uh, okay, *Mom. The Vagina Monologues* is art." This from Clarke.

And here is Kennedy, flustered. The most flustered she ever really gets. "Okay, well, can you just leave your work talk, like, at work?"

"Since when am I a gynecologist?" Clarke says. Those two. I think they've got a thing going.

"Want to come with me to the studio?" Gabe says in so low a whisper, I almost miss it.

That definitely wakes me up. The thought of Gabe dancing. "What, right now?"

"No, yesterday. *Yes*, right now," he says. His smile is so patient. So gentle. There's no intent behind it, and he's really not a huge pusher. Which is to say, he actually is just asking me if I want to join him. There is no expectation in saying yes and no harm in saying no.

That's all the thought required for me to stand, pull Gabe up with me, and throw a peace sign at the group.

Clarke sings, "Torrey and Gabey, sitting in a tree."

And, yes, because they are all five, CAKE choruses, "K-I-S-S-I-N-G!"

Cheyanne claps in a timid way that mirrors her personality, and Desh uses his thumb and forefinger to whistle louder than God at us.

I pull my hood over my head and whisper-yell, "Jesus, will y'all please shutthefuckup, it's late as hell, and I'm *too Black* to be out here making this much noise on a white college campus like that."

"Us, too," CAKE says in unison.

Do you think they practice this? Maybe they all share a brain. No, never mind. Not possible. Can absolutely admit they are the smartest people I've ever met.

Gabe slips his arm around me, pulls my back tight up against his chest, and rests his chin on the dip of my shoulder. He's laughing and carefree, and I don't know what we're all on or why or how, but I think it's a good thing. I know it's a thing I shouldn't question the way I do with everything else. And I think I can feel whatever exhale of a moment my friends live inside of all the time, whereas I only let myself watch others enjoying it.

We slip through the studio's back gate. My hand in his, he tells me the manager of the studio never locks it, for no other reason than he is dumb as rocks and that's basically it. There's another half beat of time where I think maybe I should protest and weigh the consequences of what is essentially two Black boys breaking and entering.

I don't though. And that is a victory for me.

Here, now.

We only have illumination from the lights that are intentionally left on each night but it doesn't even feel like the rest of the overhead lighting should be necessary for moments like this.

Inside, the space smells like wood. It feels softer in here, quieter and also louder in some ways.

Ducking into a small closet on the far end of the studio, Gabriel emerges a moment later, shirtless, lower half wrapped in what I think are biker shorts? And with taped feet? I'm clueless here.

Doesn't matter though, because he moves. He starts moving to no music, and then there is music. A symphony of legs, limbs. He is dance as a gale force. Gabriel Silva dances like oblivion.

And then he's spinning circles around me, brushing his fingers across my forehead in a simple hush. Silence doesn't begin to cover it when he stops moving. For a moment, I think the world is going to end if he doesn't kiss me, and I almost can't breathe with the need for it.

We are kismet: He reaches for me in the same breath that I reach for him, and then he's saving me with every promise possible, hidden inside a kiss. Promises I don't think I'll ever get from anyone else.

I press closer to him the minute I start to feel my thoughts rip him away from me. He tastes like mint, beginnings, healing, sea salt, and sunlight.

He pulls back for a moment, meets my eyes in a way that says, *It is okay.*

"I'm here. I'm right here," he says, the softest smile hidden just there. "I'm right here," he repeats, just before pressing a tear into the swell of my cheek.

I'm so used to people fucking leaving. Staying is not a thing I expect from anyone anymore. But this? I'm all in for this one, y'know?

This is an obligation I'm willing to nurture into something big. I'm willing to do the work, leave it under the sun, watch it bloom into new colors, hope it doesn't curdle.

Obligation isn't so bad when you choose it for yourself.

It's then that I know I'm staying.

I meet with Coco every morning an hour before class as mandated. It's been the same ritual for weeks now. I show up at 6:58 a.m., wait ten minutes, and then head downstairs to find her sipping coffee and reading the paper. There's literally no reason for me to show up to her lecture hall when she's not there, except maybe I think she wants me to show her that I can.

Sometimes, it feels like a game. A joke between us.

A lesson, even.

. . . Ohhhh. Oh. Okay, yeah. I get it.

After a few instances of exactly this dance, Coco has started leaving a latte and a copy of the paper on my side of the table. I always sit down to it wordlessly, flip the pages of what is honestly a well-curated student paper, pull in sips of caffeine with the same dedication I would use with a pipe.

Vices. Funny how people think I'm too young to have them. I was old enough to be left behind, to find money to keep our lights on, and to almost singlehandedly bury the man that raised me.

I'm not too young for anything anymore.

"You look stressed, mijo."

I don't know when she started calling me that, but it happened once and I didn't question it, and its been happening ever since. I feel a little bit blessed by the weight of it.

"I'm an eighteen-year-old college freshman," I say in explanation.

"Don't get cute. You know what I mean."

I do. "If I say your class is the thing that's stressing me out, do I still have to write the term paper?"

"If you say my class is stressing you out, you'll have to write two of them and turn both in next week."

I laugh but only because I know she's serious. I know Coco a little bit now and because of that, I can tell you she's absolutely not joking.

"I'm staying," I say.

"I didn't know we were leaving," she responds, eyes still glued to her paper.

Draining the last of my coffee, I say, "No. Me. I am staying. Here. Enrolled in school."

Coco glances up sharply and if I didn't know she liked me as a person before, I know it now. That much emotion from her, the way her eyebrows stand at attention. Not something I've seen in her before. She doesn't smile so much as subtly lift one side of her long mouth when she says, slowly, "That's news I'm glad to hear."

Nodding, I mumble, "Yeah. It's good." Scary and big and good.

"You let me know if that changes. You come to me, and you let me know what you need."

I should look at her, meet her stare. But I can't. Not until she demands it by throwing the balled-up wrapper of a straw at me.

"I will," I promise. And I actually feel really good about it at the time.

I'm sitting at my seat in Coco's half-circle-shaped lecture hall, the lights dim as they always are, when I pull up a webpage on my laptop in front of me. The school should have known we'd only use these things for Facebook browsing and that one oddball who watches porn in public.

Once Google loads, I type in one word: *gentrification.*

It's the first thing I think of when it occurs to me I should know what I'm looking at when this meeting with Oily Rich comes around. Figure research and preparation are the best ways to combat anxiety.

Gentrification is the very beginning of that.

In a perfect world, some jackass on the Internet is able to prove me wrong. To tell me that what's happening to the apiary and the rest of the neighborhood isn't actually gentrification, that this situation doesn't check all those boxes.

So, the first couple sources I find presuppose that I am an idiot. They're the dictionary definition of the word, the wiki link, and a geotagged government-run resource page.

Fourth on the list is the Urban Dictionary link, which I open just for shits and giggles.

The user entry says: *When a bunch of white people move to the ghetto and open up a bunch of cupcake shops.*

You are not wrong, Tucan121. You're not wrong at all.

I don't close out that tab because it's the closest I've ever come to a laugh about this situation. I know I'm supposed to be washing my hands of this whole thing. I'm aware, stop me, Susan. It's just that my hands are still technically dirty. So I'm still in this. The last thing I owe the farm is my due diligence. So I sit low in my seat, knees kissing the back of the auditorium-style seat in front of me, and I ignore Coco's lecture in favor of Google in the name of intel.

Business card out of my wallet, I type in the web address listed just under his name (the name he wishes he had). Rick Mathew.

The page opens slowly because the campus Wi-Fi is kind of trash, but once it does, I'm consumed. I'm entirely engrossed in the contents that unfold in literally the ugliest puke-mint-pastel-green color scheme I've ever seen.

His company's relatively new. They've got a ton of testimonials from people I've never heard of (not that I know anything about . . . whatever this is), Big Shot Whatever Whomevers, but I'd put a lot of money down on the fact that they're all straight, white, middle age, and male.

There is a sudden sensation of what feels like cold metal pressed to my gums and saliva pools in my mouth. I know it's a weird description, but the feeling's not new. It usually means one of two things: I am going to get a debilitating migraine, or I'm anxious.

The body's got a lot of ways of warning us when something's off. Most people ignore them. I read this study once that said if more people told their physicians about their physical responses to stress, fear, anxiety, et cetera, doctors would have three times the amount of information they do regarding how to treat those issues and disorders.

I click through to the site's contact page, through its "about" section and then on to its affiliates page.

Demolition sites.

There is a moment here when I cross over into the kind of anger there ain't no coming back from. Demolition. And I become a boy made of gravel.

I make it through all eight of the listed links, most of which boast Dick's name somewhere, noting that he's played a part in developing said companies in some capacity or another.

How? Why . . . why would he be this connected to so many of them if—

Demolition.

Shaking my head, I exhale, tired. He is going to tear down my apiary.

I swallow it down, all the exhaustion, all the hope, all the potential for bigger and better. And it's like cold metal slips down my throat impermissibly. I am helpless to catch it in exactly the same way I'd been unable to catch what was going on with the apiary in the first place.

Switching to my Messages app, I shoot one off to Gabe.

ME: I think the guy taking over the apiary lied. I think he lied to me, Gabe.

He texts back fast. *Lied like how? How do you know?*

I don't know. Not for certain. *I'm sitting in class and I Googled. Gdi Gabriel, I Googled.*

GABRIEL: I love it when you use "Google" as a verb

ME: Gabriel. He's affiliated with like, eight demolition companies and projects. His name is all over some of these websites I'm seeing! Maybe I should tell him I'm out? That I don't want to go any further.

GABRIEL: Okay, what I'm about to say to you, I say out of complete and utter adoration.

ME: I'm listening and also ready to be thoroughly offended.

He always overdoes it with the cry-laugh emojis and here, the situation's no different. *You worry too much, Torr. You're literally about to work yourself up into a serious fervor over what could totally be AND PROBABLY IS just a thing that won't apply to you. You're meeting with him to talk, right? So, talk to him. Hammer out the details, fine print, the I's and the T's or whatever when the time comes for that. Get it? Hammer. Demolition. ???*

ME: Cute. Very cute. It's my farm, though. It's Miles's and my farm. I can't just walk away from it.

GABRIEL: At all, or right now? Because, príncipe, I'm not sure you're being very honest with either of us here.

I exhale so loudly Coco's head snaps up right in my direction. "Everything okay, Torrey, or do you need to excuse yourself for some kind of deep-breathing yoga retreat?"

"Too many white people at those things, Coco."

Some of the class laughs. Coco does not.

"Yes, well. Mayhap you ought to keep some of the implied techniques to yourself. Reserve them for a later time." And then she turns back to the whiteboard and keeps lecturing.

Look, Gabriel continues. *I'm just saying, don't cross any bridges before they've even been built.*

I feel like I am quite literally in love with this boy, but he's a Pisces in every sense of the word. Free and whimsically careless in ways that both terrify and excite me because they exist in such opposition to who I am.

My email app is already up, so it's the work of a moment to shoot off an email to Ryan Q.

I don't message Gabriel back, in case that wasn't implied by the way I so quickly type out an email to the Collective's sort-of lawyer. It stands to reason that he's helped in the past and I think he can again. Right?

Yes, it does occur to me that I'm composing this email as though my laptop has offended me, cursed out my moms, and told my granmama her wig is greasy.

I get it. But that's not any kind of psychosis on my part. It's just urgency.

That, I guess, is what gentrification does. It's colonization. It's genocide. It's displacing brown people in ways that generations of their families are destroyed by. I am doing this for my uncle Miles. But I'm also doing it for the neighborhood, against all reason, sure. But the fact remains that I've got skin in the game.

Hey Q,

Torrey McKenzie. Emery's friend. With the bee farm.

Anyway, I asked her to pass along your email info and hoped you might have time—literally any time and, of course, at your leisure—to answer some questions for me? I'm pasting the link of a company below. Just want to know how much of this business is kosher, if any. I got approached by someone from this firm not long ago, and they're interested in my bees. Or, I mean. I think they are??? They say they are. That they're interested in the property, yes. But also in preserving what's already there.

Thanks for literally any help you can provide, man.

T.

I'm "studying" at the library with Gabe, which feels like a very adult thing to do. You go study. With your boyfriend. In your college campus's library.

Since I started school here, my days seem to taste less and less like childhood and more like rough decisions and their consequences. I mean, with the Add/Drop deadline having passed yesterday, I'm at a wall. An impasse. This meeting with Tiny Dick Rick *has to* go well. If it doesn't, I run the risk of having to leave school, taking an automatic fail in all my classes, thereby annihilating my GPA for any future college potential, and owing the college money.

To say the least, I'm stressin' it. And you know who can see it? Gabriel.

Whom I can feel staring at me.

Is that weird? His attention's always been like a physical sensation to me. I glance up from the $80 textbook I'm highlighting in and, yes. He is very much staring at me. The way he lifts an eyebrow, stretching his legs, all length and sinew, across the floor, is a dare if I ever saw one. And it's then I realize I am no longer peeking or glancing at him so much as staring with every possible thought running through my head made loud and clear.

"What?" I say, as if I don't know.

"I can't stare at you?" he counters, and it is the most sexual nonsexual act I've ever experienced.

I shake my head, a quick, jerky, back-and-forth thing to say *Uh, no. You may not.* Because my lips don't work properly anymore.

He chuckles to himself and goes back to studying. Aka, playing Pokémon GO on his phone for a few more minutes before he stands abruptly.

"Whoa, take it easy, Turbo."

"What?" he laughs. "Are you seventy?"

"You've been playing Pokémon for an hour on your phone. And you're talking about *my* age?"

On a stretch, he says, "Touché, jerk. I need to move." And it's so typically Gabriel that I want to squeeze him. But he starts doing this long series of . . . turns? With this, like, pointy leg-out move?

Look, whatever it is, it's goddamn beautiful.

He is goddamn beautiful.

I take out my phone and capture it on Insta story with a muttered, I'm-so-done-but-actually-so-just-getting-started, "Oh, my God." Which is about the time Gabe notices, stops, and all but sprints at me, Usain Bolt style, climbing into this very hard plastic chair with me, smacking a series of sloppy, wet, I-am-a-four-year-old kisses on me.

And I realize I'm still holding my stupid thumb down on the record button.

"Oh, shit!" I say, too loud.

The "Shhhh!" that comes back at me from somewhere in the general vicinity of the library help desk is comical.

Gabe snatches the phone from me, hops off my lap, and glances at me. "I'm posting it."

"Wait, I need content approval first, those are the rules!"

"Says who?"

"Well, it's my phone and my account, so. Me, basically."

He nods seriously. "Fair." Then, "Anyway, you can have it back now because I already did it."

"London!"

"Torrence!"

And goddammit I laugh, I can't help it. "You're the worst human I've ever met; I need to have a word with your mother about her carelessness with birth control."

"Okay whatever, masochist, you like me."

"Semantics."

"You want me."

I scoff and thank whomever-the-hell for my dark-ass skin. No human as dark as me has ever been caught blushing. "We're not having sex."

He pulls back and it dawns on me that he is still in my lap like a cat. Comfortable and proprietary. "Wait. Like, ever? Or just right now?"

"Would it be an issue if I said both?" I'm not saying both. It was just a dumb comment because there was all this implication and innuendo flying around in the air, and I got nervous and, yeah. I don't know.

"Well, no, Torr. Asexuality is a thing. I just didn't know it was *your* thing."

I shrug. "It's not. But look at you being all woke and shit."

He climbs off my lap, starts shoving books back into my bag.

"What are you doing? I'm not done studying!"

He scoffs. "You weren't studying."

Who even scoffs? No one. That's who. Not unless you're the villain in a Disney movie.

"Yes, I was."

"Yeah, okay. Sure—me."

Now I scoff. Doesn't feel right. See?

He places the bag on my shoulder before taking my hand and leading me toward the exit. He's right anyway. I wasn't studying. I was hyperfocusing on the meeting with Rick that's happening a few hours from now and getting distracted from *that* because Gabriel can't do anything unattractively for even, like, a second.

But then, immediately after Gabe's distraction, I get sucked back into stressing about this meeting and the fact that Ryan Q hasn't emailed me back yet.

I text Emery. *Heard from Q lately?*

EMERY: No, why?

Dammit.

"Torrey?" Gabe says.

"Gabriel."

"Don't say 'woke.'"

"Ironically?"

"Don't."

I laugh way too loud and another aggressive "Shhhh!" gets thrown at our backs as we hit the elevators. These people are so glad to see us leave.

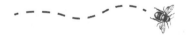

Kennedy and I are walking up to the Black Student Union to talk to someone about extra help with our shared Critical Theory paper. Marxism is a bitch. But so is MLA formatting.

It's always been easy with Kennedy. She's just my brand of quiet but not awkward, and considering who we both are as people, that's really saying something. We're both pretty big on internalizing our issues before we decide to share them.

"Helps with the delivery," Kennedy always says. "If I can just really break down things to the root of what I'm trying to say, it's easier to get it out sometimes."

Which is why, I think, we spend so much time walking toward the BSU's learning center in silence. Until Kennedy says, "I don't think I want to study programming anymore."

She's a few steps behind me, which is how Kennedy lives her life, it seems—a few steps behind but somehow still a few jumps ahead, too. "What do you mean? You want to take on some other branch of STEM?"

"Mm. No, I kind of want to look into art history."

I turn to her. "That's . . . different."

Kennedy nods, hefting her backpack higher up her shoulder. The evening classes are just starting, and the buttery lights of the campus lamps come awake slowly.

Do you ever think that your surroundings communicate with each other? I do. It feels like that now. Like, these lights maybe had a long discussion with the weather.

Ayy. We're getting real dreamy tonight, temperature.

Yeah, yeah. Soft and dreamy. You lamps, always the same.

I promise I am not high.

"I know it is," she says, a small, tentative smile pushing at her cheeks.

"Wanna tell me how you got here?"

"I've kind of always wanted to pursue art. I just didn't know how to tell the other girls that STEM doesn't do it for me like that. It's not meant to be my career. It's not a lifestyle thing for me. Coding was much better when I only did it for fun. After that, it's like, yeah, I'd really just rather not, you know?"

I do. Kind of like me and beekeeping. Did you know bees aren't born just knowing how to make honey? The younger bees are taught how to make honey by the older ones. Like unpaid bee internships.

"When is your birthday?"

"I'll be eighteen in December," she says.

Not far away. Few months from now. "Okay, well, as someone older, can I tell you something, Ken?"

She rolls her eyes as we get settled at a circular table in the BSU's lounge and wait for our student aide.

"Yes, old man. Please bless me with your wisdom."

"As someone older, I am saying to you—fuck 'em."

She drops her binder and turns to me, a laugh in her throat. "What?"

So I enunciate, "Fuck. Them."

"Not tracking."

"Listen, CAKE is CAKE because it's a more-cool-than-stupid acronym for your names, and that's it."

"Okay, go fuck yourself, though?"

"I am sorry, woman, but listen. My point still stands, I'm getting wisdom-y as shit. If your breaking away from STEM can't keep you guys the same old quad you've always been, then it wasn't going to stay that way much longer anyway. It'd mean the friendship was flimsy."

"It isn't!"

"I know it ain't! I'm just saying."

A tall redheaded girl comes to the table. She has super thick, frizzy curls and her cheeks are trying to eat up the rest of her face, but those ice blue eyes in her head are putting up a gnarly fight about it.

"Hey. I'm Spicy. Are you guys Torrey McKenzie and Kennedy Jane?"

"Yeah," I say.

Kennedy nods but is what I think people usually call punch-drunk. The way she's looking at this girl just confirms so many of my suspicions.

Kennedy is gayyyyy.

"Is Spicy a nickname, or were your parents just one of those California hippie couples who name their kids flavors they'll never remember to use in the kitchen?"

"Torrey!" Ken punches me so hard, right into one of my pecs-that-aren't-actually-pecs. I'm a beekeeper, okay? I'm not out here trying to bench press small children.

Spicy White Girl™ laughs so hard I worry that one of the veins I can see in her arms will rupture. "No," she says, sobering. "Name's actually Seraphina Spicer. Spicy for short because I don't want people thinking they can call me Sera or Seraphina."

"Spicy it is," I say. "Think you can take a look at our paper and tell us if we're on the right track?"

Fumbling much less than I figured she might, Kennedy hands Spicy our stapled ten-pager just as Spicy pulls out a chair and takes a seat next to her.

Spicy reads out loud in this weird, almost inaudible ASMR whisper.

While we're waiting for her to finish, Kennedy pulls out her phone and tries to conceal the fact that she runs a porn Tumblr. Ken is large. Ken contains multitudes.

I leave Kennedy feeling decidedly worse than I did earlier today. Anxiety eats at me, sitting just under my skin, pulsing in spots and then swimming away.

I walk and walk and don't know where I'm going. It hits me then—there's not a place on this stupid campus that feels like safety or solid ground beneath my feet.

Except, maybe, for Gabriel. Wherever he is, I feel like I'm at my most calm.

The walk to his dorm is even farther than the walk to my own dorm. But it's necessary. It's basically dark now and those lights are still buttery but with a little more flare now, and my footsteps aren't at all memorable. Which is how I come to find myself at the door to Gabe's room, just sort of standing in front of it like it's Platform 9¾.

Geek reference, I know. I'm not above that, though, and neither are you.

The door whooshes open after maybe a minute. Possibly two. And Gabe's there holding a highlighter-pink flyer in his hand.

Looks like someone made it on their mother's 1997 version of Microsoft Paint.

"Hi," Gabe says. He's so happy and God, just . . . so damn lovely, if that is a word I am even allowed to use. He's lovely without even trying, which only makes him all the more so.

Like, the way he pulls the corner of his bottom lip in with his teeth. Or the way he scrunches his nose up sometimes, the picture of adorable confusion. It's the angles of his jaw plus his almost-feminine mouth. He's the most explosive combination of brazen sexuality and unacknowledged innocence I've ever seen in a person.

I'm dating a baby Adonis.

Gabe presses a firm kiss right up under my jaw.

"Príncipe?" he asks, tugging on the hem of my shirt. "What happened? What's wrong?"

He's pulling me inside and I don't know how I'm supposed to get words out right now. I don't feel like myself. Not unless he's touching me. So I squeeze his hand and beg him with my touch to be my anchor to this reality.

What I'm about to discuss with Richard Mathew in just under two hours is big. So much bigger than me or anything I should be allowed to handle.

I wish I could just get there and be done with it now.

"Lisa?" Gabriel says. "Theo? Did something happen to Theo?"

I shake my head, seated on his bed now. I think I'm sitting on the flyer, so I pull it onto my lap to find the flyer's still in his hand, too. So now his hand is in my lap and all I can do is stare at it and shake my head as he runs a list of people who are important to me.

"Your mom? Lisa? Are you sure it's not Lisa? Mrs. Xu, Mr. Jones? God, Torr, you're *scaring* me."

And that—that very thing right there—*you're scaring me*—that's the thing that wakes me up.

"No, I'm fine. Just tired and overwhelmed and anxious about this meeting and also aggressively sure I'm about to bomb this critical theory paper." Should I add a laugh in there for good measure?

No time for a vote—I do it anyway. A good self-deprecating one, too.

He runs an unsure hand up and down the front of my neck, down to my collarbones, fingers splayed. "Príncipe. You would tell me, wouldn't you?"

"If there were something to tell, yeah. Always."

He whispers, "Okay," and presses his mouth to mine, whispering, again, just to be sure I've heard it and felt it, "Okay."

"What's this?" I say, shaking the paper in both our hands.

It really is the ugliest flyer I've ever seen. Jesus.

"There's this thing called an Undie Run. It's later on tonight. Let's go."

I give him a look. Just one lifted brow.

"Yeah," he says, "Let's go. We can go be goofballs and take your mind off of things. Just let loose, y'know? It'll be good. Good for all this." He gestures at me.

Skeptical, I ask, "What is it?"

He shakes the flyer in my face, leaning all his weight into me. "What it sounds like, ya goober. You run around campus in your underwear with, like, a bunch of other people."

I stare at him. *Goober.*

"I don't know! It sounds like fun to me."

I shake my head and ask, "People run for fun?"

"Apparently so."

"You understand that when a group of people is running away from something, it's usually bad, and Black people don't typically stop to ask questions. We just haul ass and book it in whatever direction everybody else is going."

"I'm sorry, are you explaining Blackness—Black culture to me? Of all people?"

Ahh. Slippery slope with him. Gabe's one trigger when we were kids was the not-Black-enough debate. His dad is Black. Like, Black as it gets. Like, Blackity-Black. Like, this-country-owned-your-ancestors Black. His mom's Brazilian. Still ID's as Black, but primarily Afro-Latina.

Look, okay—it was a whole thing. For Gabriel—for London, a greener, newer heart—it mattered. It was a discussion he got so tired of having with people.

Not one I could understand, really. So I just listened. It was really all he wanted. Someone to listen to him while he called them all bitches in his cracking, barely-there puberty voice. Identity politics is a hell of a thing for a thirteen-year-old to have to digest.

"I'm sorry," I say to him now. "You're right. I don't have to and never have had to explain that kind of shit to you. Let's meet up here later and then we'll go. Yeah?" I press up against him, no hands, and then kiss him because I'm not sure how else to say I'm sorry.

He nods, quiet.

"Yeah?" I say again.

"Mm-hmm." He runs his lips across the apple of my cheek, inhales. It's ocean ripples, growing wider until they're no more. It's natural.

Words . . . am I perpetuating the stereotype if I say I'm no good at them? Never have been. I just never learned that stuff and exploring it wasn't an option.

Quit bein' a sissy, boy, ain't nobody tryna be up in here talking about your delicate-ass feelings. Out here crying like a little girl. Go sit your ass on the porch then if you need to be emotional so bad.

Theo made sure I never got a chance to touch it. And no one ever corrected him. Not Miles, not Lisa, not Moms when she was around. Not the neighbors or old Ms. Ollie down at the corner beauty supply that time Theo made me go with him to buy a new hair pick and caught me looking at some of the earring studs.

Which is ironic.

I kiss Gabriel because, instead, my family tried to teach me that expressing emotions was non-masculine.

Two masc dudes kiss to express feelings that homophobia tried to rob them of.

Write that tell-all.

When he pulls away, he presses his forehead to mine. "Let's just stay in."

I shake my head. "No. No, we should go. It does sound fun. Plus, if you wear your Spider-Man briefs, I'll wear my Batman ones."

"The ones with the bat over the crotch?"

"Yes, and BAT SIGNAL right across the ass."

He's excited. I've made him happy. For a second, I am a college kid just trying to figure out how to coordinate underwear with my boyfriend—how to have a relationship with another person at all—and that feeling stays with me all the way up until I leave his dorm room to go change into the aforementioned mammal-crotch boxer briefs at my own dorm.

I'm pulling the briefs up and settling them around my hips, running scenarios through my head about this meeting with Mathew when my phone does that double buzz that means I've an email waiting. I open it up to find Ryan Q has emailed me back, finally. I haven't been waiting long, but it just feels like twenty-four hours is much longer than it actually is when you're waiting on something like this.

Torrey,

Hey. Sorry about the delay. I'm sleep deprived and stacked on shit I have to do, but I know Emery would probably castrate me if I dropped the ball on this for you, so thank her and let her know how much I came through for you.

That said, uhh, this guy is a fucking Sketch McGetch. Like, in a big way. I'm gonna link you to some articles I found that basically map out how this guy just jumps from business to business and has been totally infamous for orchestrating these low-key deals that backfire for the other parties involved.

The companies he has listed at the bottom of his site aren't ALL his, but he owns a percentage of enough of them that he could black-ball each and still turn some kind of profit. There's even one that's local to SF. They just started working with the company that bought up that one restaurant in the Tenderloin.

Torrey, hear me right now.

Do not do business with this dude. He's oily, bro. Dude's a modern-day mobster with the way he's sliding in and out of legal hang-ups. His MO seems to be that he's been tearing up neighbor-hoods block by block and doing it through some super not-right deals. Deals that he's reneged on. Some of the people in these deals have even tried to sue him, but none of their suits ever stick, and the ones that do often just get a settlement and then they're closed.

Better safe than sorry if you care about your family's property at all.

Let me know if I can answer any other questions for you.

Good luck out there.

RQ

Shit.

Shit shit shit!

Abruptly, I'm on my feet, reaching into my back pocket for a worn, familiar business card.

His voicemail picks up. "You've reached the offices of Rick Mathew. Leave your name—spelled twice, slowly—and a contact number, and I'll return your call at my earliest convenience. For a more immediate response, please email me at R dash M at R dash Mathew Corp dot com."

And when that damn beep sounds, I go ape shit all over his voicemail.

Spell your name twice, slowly my ass. I'm not spelling shit.

"Hey, Dick!" Off to a great start here, aren't we. "Torrey Aloysius McKenzie, here. I'm sure you won't have any trouble spelling that. So listen, I've got some interesting information for you. Yeah, found it in an article. On the Internet, where information goes, not to die, but to be preserved in sixteen-point Comic Sans on local eNews sites."

Here's a little from one such article:

A California property management company is under investigation for allegedly collecting rent from its tenants and failing to pay property-tax owners.

"Numerous complaints have been filed against R & M Management of Central California Properties and its owner, Richard-Fucking-Mathew."

I definitely improv'd that last bit. Seems they don't know your nickname preferences either, *Dick*.

"Here's what I'm getting at: I know you own a ton of management companies across the fucking country. I know more than half are twice as oily as your pasty-ass forehead. I know you've been kissing my ass while trying to finesse me out of this property so you can eventually just screw us over the same way you always have and put a Whole Foods or a . . . a, I don't know . . . a fucking kombucha factory in its place.

"Well, fuck you very much, dickhead, I'll give you hell at every turn and Black people don't even like Whole Foods, we're Trader Joe's people. And, to make sure you really feel me, I need you to know that you won't ever touch a single bee on my property. Consider this my cancellation of our meet-up later. You played yourself. Congratulations."

And I turn around after hanging up, phone clenched tightly in my hand, because if I loosen my grip on it at all, it's going to get hurled against one of the walls in this hallway.

I'm shaking. It's never going to end. I can't stay here, and it was so dumb of me to think it'd be this easy to wash my hands of it. To have my cake and eat it, too.

God, I should have listened to Emery.

Moms used to always say, "Hard head makes a soft ass."

Yeah, no kidding. Patricia McKenzie is right about some things, apparently.

I throw my clothes back on, step-by-step, my movements feeling mechanical and almost subconscious.

Black jeans, one leg at a time, following a black long-sleeved thermal, a black sweatshirt, and the only beanie that sat just on the floor near the door. One by one, clothes go on instead of coming off, and I find myself rummaging through the giant trunk at the end of Desharu's bed to find a can of black spray paint.

And then, nothing on my mind but my uncle and my neighborhood, my feet carry me left, off campus, instead of right, toward the beautiful boy waiting for me in his dorm room.

I have a bus to catch.

It's the last thing I think before I leave.

Gabriel's nowhere in any of it.

'm going to the site. Of course I'm going to the site.

Half a dozen times, I manage to talk myself in and out of whatever it is I'm about to do, can of spray paint clutched in my hand.

The property is located in Pleasanton, California.

Pleasanton is like if East LA's younger, more pretentious cousin came home from boarding school and had to move in with you and your family.

Pleasanton would use the term "ghettoized" to refer to the body wash in your shower.

Pleasanton would tell you they got the same bamboo earrings

you got. But from Urban Outfitters. Two years ago.

Pleasanton is the Bay Area hood for hipsters. Pleasanton's God—its creator—is gentrification.

Which is why I'm exactly 0 percent surprised that it is the location of this construction site. The shop that used to be here was, according to what debris still remains, a diner called Corazón. You can guess at the owners it probably displaced.

It's never not some Black or brown people.

The construction site looks a little like oblivion.

In an effort to illuminate the city's crime, streetlights around the site are stacked far too close together, a copse of leafless trees and their orange orb branches. Fog has rolled in slowly, whispering along the cracked dirt gravel like a secret waiting to be buried.

Pillars and steel beams stacked like Tetris have converged on the small space in question. Tractors covered in mud and black streaks of what I assume to be oil sit positioned in groups of two, dead like toy robots down on battery life.

Here, in this part of town, couples still have arguments with the windows open and tíos and tías still dance bachata on the porch with the sound up on its highest setting, but only because they don't know any better yet.

The city hasn't taught them that Black and brown people get fined for expressing emotions at a volume white people find to be *too much*.

There's a brick wall all the way in back that's covered in white banners with red lettering.

FUTURE HOME OF YOUR NEW SoMa!

SoMa. South of Market.

Over it, I spray paint BY ANY MEANS NECESSARY, the can kicking in my hand with the first vertical line of the B, smoothing out as I hit the Y, the A, the N, and so on. Done, I finish it off by tagging an X just below it, demanding they pay attention, the way Malcolm would have wanted it.

This area is basically a neighborhood that's been built primarily for immigrant families and low-income housing. According to some of the information Q sent, the plans for this are to create more jobs and less viable housing for those families.

The ones already here will be forced out with a jump in rent prices and the balance of available work will skew given the amount of employees who would have to commute all the way from places like Oakland.

It's everywhere, this gentrification shit. It's careless and it escapes me how people—white people who have never been and will never be affected by this—would fail to explore all avenues and future points of downfall.

I know, I know. I'm not being naive here. They don't give a shit, and if it keeps Black and brown folks under a shoe then their work has been done.

Systemic oppression.

Google it. Spend forty-five minutes reading articles written by Black people.

Then come back and tell me you wouldn't pick up the

crowbar like I have now.

Tell me you wouldn't put every ounce of hurt and anger and frustration that's ever touched your body into that first swing. Tell me you wouldn't double down on it with the second. Tell me your third, fourth, and fifth swings wouldn't pull on your muscles like fire.

Mine all do. A score, settled.

And they don't stop there. I take the crowbar to every damageable piece of equipment that dares to find me, and the reverberation of the metal-against-metal strikes skip up my arms and settle right in my elbows.

In my chest, I feel a scream that knows it has to stay put, but I can't help that with every new piece of equipment I dent, there's a small growl, a release that demands to be given a voice.

They say there are people called synesthetes who, on occasion, experience emotion as color. I've never believed in that kind of thing.

Not until now, when a haze of red becomes the feeling of knowing, of helplessness. Blinding white bleeds in every time reason tries to pull my arm back, only to be forced out by red

and red

and red

and red

red, then blue, and both together in a jumping dance of colors that finally registers as something outside of me and what I can feel.

The small blip of sound that infiltrates is a surge of nitrogen in my blood.

Police.

It's ironic that this fear seems to come at me in a familiar color. Black.

"**D**rop your weapon!"

Three words have never in my life been so confusing and so incredibly clear.

The metal of the crowbar bites into my palm as I reflexively squeeze it tighter. I try—I try repeatedly—to let it go. To drop it. And I know in my head and chest that this is the weapon they're referring to, but fear tightens my grip and denies every response my brain tries to send in the name of self-preservation.

"Drop your damn weapon and get down on the ground."

An image of Uncle Miles swims into my vision, right there, front and center, and that's all I need. My entire body convulses, crowbar falling to the ground in almost the same instant as my knees hit the dirt, rocks and debris cutting into my skin, right through my jeans.

I'm already facedown on the ground, still convulsing, shaking so violently that I bite my tongue, and there's really no guarantee that I haven't bitten it clean in half. I'd almost suspect that I have by the way my face starts to hurt, but soon there's no doubt in my mind that it's a new pain altogether.

A knee in my back. A hand pressed into my face so hard that I feel a rock cut into my cheek, and what I suspect is a shoe meeting the back of my skull—a combination made to rob me of everything but what is raw inside me, so that it's all I have left.

They take everything from me. They do it so that they have a reason.

I call out several times, so many times, so many, though I'm not sure any of it is actual words. I'm down and not resisting, I'm not resisting just the way Uncle Miles and Moms and Lisa and Theo and Mr. Jones and every other Black adult in my life have instructed me not to. I'm not resisting, I'm doing my best, and it's not good enough for them because I feel it, I feel the kiss of cold steel at the back of my head, right up against my scalp, my hat gone in a forceful swipe that stings in a way that mimics how my eyes feel, stinging with dirt and sweat and tears that I fucking wish to God I'd been able to keep to myself. This, a violation in itself, robs me of everything, and I wish, I keep wishing that I'd been able to save some of myself from being snatched by them.

I don't know whether it's better to keep quiet or to talk—to promise them that I hear what they're demanding, that a gun in my skull isn't necessary, that I'm not resisting, I'm not resisting, I promise I'm sorry I'm not resisting, that I'm a good person—that I am a person.

I feel so small. And I lose myself in that feeling. I lose myself and who I am, and giving up, that's always felt unfathomable until now.

It feels real now, so real that I can admit that I've always known there were many of us in this, many of us Black boys who get hit here, while still—still, you do nothing.

Hands up.

Don't shoot.

I can't breathe.

I'm not resisting.

These words will mean nothing to you. But they mean everything to us.

C uffs.
   The back of the police car.
A dragging march, point A. Point B.
Holding.
Processing.
Holding.
Holding.

I don't know how long they're allowed to deny me this, but I don't get a phone call. Not until what I estimate to be several hours later. The circle clock on the wall hasn't moved its arms even once since I've been here.

But then I do get my call. And she's there. Here. Lisa's here, and she's a mess. She is sobbing and wordless, and she is shaking. And forgetting this image of her . . . it's going to be a slow unraveling.

It feels weird that she doesn't touch me once I've been released and given all my personals and stuff. She barely even looks at me as we walk out the door of the station and out into the parking lot.

When she does finally stop in her tracks and turn to me, it's to hit me. Like, I am not super tall, but I am taller than Lisa. By a good amount. But Black women in a chaotic explosion like this . . . it's dangerous. She slaps at and punches me in the chest repeatedly, and all I can do is let her. All I can do is let it happen until she exhausts herself. I did this to her, and I hate it. Hate knowing I turned her into this person who can't communicate how she feels through her words and has to resort to using her fists instead because it hurts so much to be reminded of the system, to be reminded of the status quo and how it ended the life of the man you love with your entire self.

When you see something like this on TV or in movies and the other person just has to stand there and take it and then they become this human straitjacket. That's real.

It happens in real life because there is literally nothing else to do but that.

"This has to stop, Torrey. It has to stop!"

I nod and hold her tight. And tighter and tighter and tighter still as she yells.

"They could have killed you. They would have killed you, Torrey, there was no reason for them not to. Do you understand what I am saying to you?" She meets my stare and it's so clear that she's begging me, eyes searching, *to just get it*. Because she cannot and will not be able to verbalize it.

"I need you to really hear me when I say this. Listen very carefully. Miles would not have wanted this for you. He'd have burned the farm to the ground first before he ever let you be handcuffed over it."

"I know," I say, even knowing I shouldn't. I don't know what else to say though.

I gambled with my life.

"Do you? You're an adult! They could charge you as an adult. And more importantly, you could have been shot dead. Tonight. You could have been killed. You are worthless to them, Torrey. They look at you—they see an animal. One of a number of problems with a heartbeat and nothing more."

Help. Please, help me, I can't keep feeling this way.

"I know," I say. I can't help it. My only other option is to say the truth. That I understand just how many people on this planet would rather I didn't exist. And that, sometimes, I wish I didn't either. So I just keep repeating the same thing: "I know, I know that."

I'm barely able to catch my breath now, bubbles popping after existing a moment—maybe less.

And I'm breaking into so many pieces.

Please help me. I don't know how to live this way.

I know that my worth, my value, has never been much of anything. Never will be. Not in my lifetime and probably not in the next either.

Finally, I offer, "I'm sorry." And she just squeezes me so tight in reply.

The car ride back to campus is so quiet. Aunt Lisa doesn't let go of my hand, and when the circulation in it is clearly being cut off and I try to pull away, she holds tighter and says, only, "I can't. Just a little longer."

"Okay," I say, if only to just verbalize something. "Yeah, that's okay."

When we arrive, she parks in the student lot and cuts the engine.

"Is this a rental?" I say. Lisa drives Uncle Miles's manual '03 Honda Civic. It's a good car. But this . . . is not that. This is a fucking Hyundai.

"Yeah. I just didn't want to be stuck waiting on an Uber. Plus, the airport has good deals."

"I'll pay you back for the flight." I know this isn't money she had to spare.

"Boy, shut up. Don't nobody want your forty-eight dollars."

Smiling feels like a thing people write songs about but don't actually do in real life. Feels new and uncomfortable.

"Are you going back tonight?"

Aunt Lisa hits a switch to roll the windows down and let some fresh air in that doesn't taste like tears.

"I booked a one-way, so I might just drive back whenever."

Not an answer. "What about where you're staying? Hotel? Airbnb?"

"My dad has some cousins who live in the Mission."

I nod. "Cousins you know?" Lisa isn't super tight with her dad. She's my family. I'd sooner have her sleeping in the dorm with me and Desh than some whack-ass place that feels foreign to her.

She nods back. "The only good thing about his side of the family."

"You eat?"

"Torrey, I swear to God, if you don't stop trying to Black Mom me to death, boy."

Here—here is where the smiling thing becomes more acquaintance than stranger.

"Get out of my car, Torr. I hear there's a boy in there waiting for you."

I hug her and try to communicate that she is the strongest oak tree. That she is never not blooming and bursting from the ashes.

She's right. Gabriel is waiting for me just inside the door of Prominski, seated in one of those itchy, reupholstered-one-time-too-many chairs they're constantly redecorating the first-floor commons with.

"How'd you know?" I say.

He uncrosses his legs in this way, just so, how only a dancer would. "How'd I know you were going all stealth burglar with a death wish? I didn't. Not at first. But you didn't show up to the Undie Run, and then your phone kept going to voicemail when I called you, and that literally never happens, so I ended up having to get super creepy and tracking you on Find My Fucking Friends—which I will probably not forgive you for making me do, Torrey—and basically it just took some Googling from there. And . . . also, I called the apiary and had to leave a message on their answering machine and apparently your friend Endira gets all voicemails transcribed to her email? And she gave Lisa my number?"

Wow.

"Wow. Uh . . . that was a lot."

"You're damn right it was a lot. It was a lot for me to have to go through. Jesus, Torrey, what the hell. Why couldn't you just have talked to me or to Lisa or to literally any of the billions of people who care about you before deciding to fly off the freaking handle?"

I pace. It's all I can do. It's late enough—or, rather, early enough—that I can't really go all Rambo on him in this dorm lounge. "You're one to talk."

"What?"

"You're talking to me about flying off the freaking handle? You? Mr. Rules don't apply to me, Mr. Run around campus after hours in your underwear, Mr. Break into your dance studio. Gabriel, you are the literal embodiment of flying off the handle. You are made up of carelessness, and that's just not who I am."

"You're judging me like you weren't in that stuff with me."

"I was in it with you because I am in love with you, not because I wanted to or needed to."

"Great, so, hard-up, can't-ever-make-a-move Torrey is right, and I'm just wrong."

"I'm not saying you're wrong for all that. Stop putting words in my mouth. What I am saying is that you are wrong to judge me and try to make me out to be some kind of screw-up all because I did something radical for a reason that actually matters and not just because I wanted to be some kind of manic pixie dream boy."

That's it. All of it. This is how we end.

Gabriel and I are each other's antonyms. There's no denying or fixing that fact. If even I can't make sense of this thing between us, how many more people are rooting against us because the math of him and me doesn't add up?

He stands. I can tell his fight-or-flight reservoir is all out of fight. "All I'm asking is for you to bend a little, Torr."

"And all I'm asking for is that you take something—anything—seriously for once."

I regret it immediately. My grams used to tell us, "It's not what you say, it's how you say it."

I think what I just said and how I said it—neither is okay. He proves me right when he shakes his head, glances at me long enough for me to catch the tears in his eyes, and then leaves without another word.

*I*n my dorm room, the lights are all off when I walk in, but one of Emery's oil diffusers is in the corner serving as a night-light.

I stop short when I take in the sight of all my friends scattered around the room.

Do they know? They have to. They know what happened, and they did this for me.

Do they know how much I love them? They did this for me, so maybe they do.

My girl is the only one awake when I walk in. "We're using an essential oil for calming since none of us could manage it on our own," Emery says.

I hug her. Hug her so tight and thank God this girl calls me friend. Sometimes it's just enough to be found worthwhile to one person who is clearly a better human than you'll ever be.

Clarke and Auburn are splitting my bed, while Kennedy and Emery share Desh's, which is funny because these standard dorm-issue beds are barely large enough for *one* adult-size body, let alone two. Desh's sleeping situation is probably the winner—he's starfished on the floor right there in the middle, which is pretty much also how he lives his life.

Emery rearranges Kennedy into a position where the three of us can lay horizontally on Desh's bed. It's not comfortable, but it is comforting.

It's the safest I've felt in a long time. It's hard not to wonder how a person could feel so many different emotions all arm-wrestling one another for the top spot.

Comforted, safe, lonely, alone.

It's probably why so much of my struggle with the apiary has been what it is, this constant pull back and forth between who I am and who I could be, what I want, what I need, and what I think others want or need from me.

I've been fighting with myself for a very long time, and Uncle Miles is the one person who helped me win that fight. He didn't try to stop me—just gave me the tools to succeed. I think he understood, better than I ever will, that sometimes the fight is necessary. It always gets you to the other side and at the end of it, you'll always have picked up something new, regardless of the fight's outcome: a couple new bruises or some bragging rights.

Both of which can be valuable in the hands of a Black boy.

And so now—now, when people want to take the apiary from me, it's like they're trying to take Miles from me. And if they succeed there, then what am I? Who am I? Who do I become when he's really and truly gone?

Taking my bees means taking my uncle away, and taking him away means losing the piece of myself he helped me to be.

Still . . . did I go too far tonight? Am I fighting a battle that doesn't need to be fought? Is winning this one going to be good for me?

Maybe I'll win. Maybe I'll get to keep my farm and my bees. And then what? Where will I be, now that the Add/Drop deadline has come and slipped right by me while I was busy being absent and in love?

I cannot keep things together all the way from San Francisco. I really can't.

It starts in my hands. My right hand, first. The tremors. It forces me to grab the shaking hand with my steady one, but it's no use because then the left is shaking and I feel it starting to take up all the room in my chest that isn't being inhabited by the way my heartbeats have multiplied and rippled out like a riot with a message to tell.

That's what's happening. My body is telling the story of my last forty-eight hours.

My body is reliving it all.

"Cut me out of this place."

"Torrey?" Emery says. I don't realize I've said it out loud. Am still saying it out loud. Not until I feel Em wrap her arms around me from behind. She grips me so tight that it starts to feel like I just might unthaw. But then the tremors wreck me all over again, and I curl up into the fetal position. I try and try and try, alone and far from home, stuck in one place and chained to another, to convince myself I'm not in over my head.

I am.

"Breathe, Torrey."

I am. I am.

"Torrey. You have to breathe."

I am!

I'm so desperate for anyone to fix it. I just want to sleep all this life away.

God, do I lack the common sense to let go of a thing that's practically killing me with a smile on its face? I'm out of my mind.

Face pressed into the mattress, I swallow a scream. What else is left? What else is there?

She shakes me a little and then bites, *"Torrey"* right into my ear, and I feel it like a crack, feel it just as roughly as I feel each of the bruises I earned tonight.

"Breathe," she says again.

I whisper, "I am."

All along I've thought, no matter what it takes, I'm going to make sure no one so much as sneezes the pollen off a single bee on that farm. It's like I needed to fight for them the way nobody but Miles ever fought for me. But through all that, I think maybe I missed the fact that I am losing pieces of myself in order to protect pieces of myself.

How much of that is worth it?

I feel like, no matter what I decide, I am never going to be whole. I am, right now, shaking so hard that pieces of me are falling off, moment by moment.

There is no real fixing or repairing. Only choosing. There is only choosing.

I should have known things weren't one hundred percent copacetic when, the week after my brief love affair with vandalism and nervous breakdowns, I have still heard nothing from Oily Rick or his company. We were told as I was leaving the station that night that no charges were being held against me.

There was no bone in my body that didn't want to question that.

Lisa, on the other hand, looked at me, pointed at the police officer and said, "That is what you call a gift horse, stupid. Let's go."

So, suffice it to say, I didn't ask any questions.

But that's usually where things trip me up. When I don't ask the questions I know I should. It happens to me in Coco's class, it happens to me when I'm buying discount bread from the grocery store, and so yeah, in this, when I should have questioned the whys of it, and then didn't . . . well. That's probably why Oily Rick is here. At my dorm, again, following me into the commons.

I hate having conversations here. It's official.

"You're welcome," he says, smile on his face. It occurs to me then and there that sharks—as in, the species of fish—do not smile.

"Whatever," I say. Then, under my breath, "Greasy head-ass motherf—"

"I didn't catch that."

"I said, 'Whatever'. Stop following me, please. Stalking is highly frowned upon."

"So's vandalism."

"Is it?" Jackass.

"Look, son."

"I'm not your son."

"My company . . . we're not pressing charges. Why? Because I'm a charitable guy."

Or because Ryan Q pulled up hella dirt on him and his back channel–ass businesses. But I digress.

"I am, however, here to tell you that you've essentially just screwed yourself. Not a huge chance you're going to get to keep your farm with that little demolition project you orchestrated. Now your petition amounts to nothing more than scratch paper and some illegible names of people who don't matter much now."

Breathless. That's what this does to me, it seeps in and commandeers my breath.

He smiles again. I hate him. I hate it. I hate everything about this. "See you at auction, son." He chucks my chin with a finger, turns, and walks away.

Two mornings later, I find myself at a local coffee and wine bar called Hostel.

Hostel is one of the places I've basically fallen head over heels with here in San Francisco. Not unlike a certain Afro-Latino boy made up entirely of hair and stardust.

Hostel is relatively new, but it's designed to basically look like a squat bunker with black walls and exposed brick. But there's stuff to like about this try-hard imperfection. Like the way the bathroom door's handle sometimes locks on you, and you have to give it a real good hip check before it agrees to let you out.

Or the way the Wi-Fi goes out every time the fog decides to move with a little gusto, requiring a reset within ten minutes' time, or else the on-duty supervisor will be stuck on the phone with Time Warner Cable.

Emery walks in.

I'm shoving a paperback into my back pocket and walking toward her when she nods in the other direction, and heads to the corner of the commune dedicated to Collective business.

An idea starts to take shape. One that, if executed properly—and within the next two weeks—could save the apiary.

Since the Collective is a group of activists based in LA city proper, it's a big deal that they're here, in the Bay. They're not so much run by any one person as they are a tentative group of lost boys. Think Occupy, but Black and based on the opposite coast.

They're big on the usual things—pushing back against anti-Islamic rhetoric, BLM, the influx of ICE raids that've been taking place of late as well as funding causes like the Latino Victory Project and Planned Parenthood. But they also do the small things. They are single-handedly responsible for funding the lunch program at six out of the nine local elementary and middle schools in the LA area. They're feeding kids whose parents can't afford the lunch program. Some of these kids—it's the only meal they get in a single day, and if that ain't good work, don't tell me what is.

I walk toward their group, huddled in a circle. The stress is palpable. Hands on chins, brows lowered—something's happened.

Em looks up at me. Nods as she speaks to the group. "No. You know that's not how we operate. Our project is proactive and visionary—not reactive. We don't fight fires just because they're blazing and we happen to have a couple of red cups of water in hand. Leave that to others who have the power to do so. Our fight is with the embers it leaves behind and the sparks that ignited it in the first place."

Before I walk away, I glance down and see flyers on each of their laps for what they intend to be the first annual Foster Care and Adoption Awareness Rally.

"The whole point of this," Emery continues loud enough for her circle and even me to hear, "is to help Black youth see how they can get in on the ground level. How they can be more active in things like the Collective."

A kid with too much hair on top of his head rises. The tips are bleached so there's, like, a 70 percent chance he's going to say something dumb. He's familiar. I've seen him around LA, on the west side, I think.

"We just lost two of our sponsors due to these assholes coming in and shutting down our event site. What are we supposed to do about that now? *We don't have a venue, Emery!*"

She sits down, and I silently beg her not to give up. *Don't concede.* I so selfishly want her to fight for this thing she loves and believes in. We're alike in a lot of ways and one of them, I know, is that we were given too much passion to hold inside our bodies. And now, the object of my passion is all fight and very few moments of love.

I've known Em for the duration of my stay here at SFSU, but I wouldn't say I know her well enough to bet on her next move. But it just doesn't seem like her MO to just give up once one obstacle is set gently in her path.

She seems like the type to *maybe* concede on a temporary basis once the fiftieth obstacle is dropped like an anvil. But nothing short of that.

I clear my throat. "Use us. Or, me. Or, damn. I mean, like—"

"Spit it out, bruh," Frosted Tips says.

I give him a look but Emery slaps him across the back of the head before I can say anything.

"Thanks," I say to her. "I meant that you guys can use the apiary for your rally. My farm," I clarify for Vanilla Ice over there. "It's private property, so at least there's that."

"I like the idea of that," Emery says. "Doing it in the city would be so baller and having an actual space to do it on-slash-around would be perfect."

"We don't have that kind of money. I know what it takes to rent a space that size." This, from a guy with red lipstick and a badass, anatomically correct heart tattooed on his neck.

He's probably right about their money situation though. We've rented out the apiary to about a handful of private parties in the past, garden parties, wine tastings, baby showers where we've had more than a few stings because some idiot father-to-be couldn't keep his hands to himself. Point is, we're not cheap because it takes money to keep us going.

"Yeah," I say, readjusting my stance. "But I'm willing to forego the cost. I need this just as much as you guys do. This is important, and it's not about money. And the city councilman's office is like four blocks east of the farm."

She exhales. "Do you know what you're asking for? Because we're all on board, but there are risks involved."

"I think so, but I'm sure you'll correct me if I get it twisted. I need protest. The Collective needs action. We combine the two and meet them at the top. At the councilman's office. I need to show them there's genuine support and pushback as a result of shutting us down. And they need to know we know our rights. Black lives don't matter to them, and I understand that they especially won't while we're there, raising hell."

"You've done your homework."

"I know my way around Google, yeah."

She nods. "This isn't the kind of thing that just comes together overnight. You know that, right? It takes weeks of planning and coordinating. Sometimes months."

I nod, even though I'd hoped to have it pulled together at sort of an expedited rate.

"Has to be two weeks. My farm is yours if we can make this happen by then." It has to. "And, in the event y'all end up needing to hold another rally, I'm pretty sure I know a rec center that'd be willing to jump in. I can make that happen."

I think. I'm not entirely certain, but I'll promise anything to damn near anyone right now. Plus, I've worked with the rec center long enough to know they've thrown their support behind lesser causes for people a lot less deserving than the Collective's members.

She exhales, then mumbles, "Freakin' tired."

I know, right. You, too? Yeah. This life shit's for the birds, ain't it?

I pull her aside to a far corner of the room and lower my voice. "I know this probably only adds to what stress you already have going, but I just really want you to know I'm not going to take advantage of what you can do or can offer. I'm willing to help you and the Collective out, too. Beyond just this. If you help me hang onto it, my space is yours for whatever you need. Rallies, fundraisers, events, parties, meetings. Hell, I've seen that kid with the Y2K Justin Timberlake hair sleeping in his car from time to time. There's a bed in the apiary's back shed that's his for whenever he wants it, so long as you can give me your word he's not gonna try and pawn my espresso machine or anything."

This time she does laugh. "Yeah, Justice has a space to sleep, it's just. He was adopted last year."

"Kinda late in the game for a Black kid, isn't it?"

"Late in the game for anyone to be adopted, yeah. But. He's not comfortable with them yet. Doesn't believe they want him for real. Which. They might not, but they signed the adoption papers, so there's gotta be some genuine desire there. Anyway, he tells them he's staying at a friend's place and then takes off and sleeps in his car instead."

"If they signed the papers and made it official, what's even in it for them?"

"I don't know. Street cred? Respectability?"

"They're a white family?" I ask. It's the only way I can see around something like that.

"No," she says. "Asian. They're, like, second-gen Korean."

I nod. "Lot of politics in that." The history of Black and Asian interpersonal relationships is . . . messy.

"Yeah," she says.

"So," I say.

"So," she says.

"Will you help me put this thing together with some quickness, a little finesse?"

She hangs onto her answer for a second, and I know she's making me wait because that's just my Emery—exacting. And utterly incomparable.

I groan, "Put me out of my misery, Em."

"Whatever. Yes, I'll help get this thing off the ground in a hurry."

"Yes!" I hug her and it's probably a mistake. Confirmed! When she suddenly decks me right in the chest. "Christ, Em. These are new," I say holding my chest. "My plastic surgeon is going to be furious."

"You're such a dweeb."

I smile. Feels pretty cool. "Thanks, shorty."

She folds her arms across her chest and mulls for a moment, lips sliding from one side of her mouth to the other.

"What?" I say.

"My mind's already dancing around how we can get this ball rolling."

"Deadass. I've been thinking maybe we need an online presence to really reach people."

"Okay," she says. "Online presence like what? A webpage? A GoFundMe? A newsletter? All of the above?"

"That one."

"Mm. I got you. Whatever you need, okay? You're a pain in my ass, Torr, but I got you."

She and I set up a Twitter page and the GFM pretty much on the spot, because technically winning this fight over the apiary has to end in us paying those back taxes, even if we do stop the auction.

As soon as she splits, she's already texting me with possible options for a hashtag we can use online to get some chatter going.

#SavetheBeesLA

#Action4Apiary

#MilesToGoApiary

That feeling . . . did you catch it, too? It was quick, so I'll tell you—it's akin to that of a wildfire.

Whenever I'm having a particularly hard time, I end up in the same place. If not physically, then mentally.

Today Moms has a flower in her hair. It finally hits me that she is aging. Death is a different sort of thing when your loved one has been on a ventilator for as long as Moms has. I'm so used to having her be at death's whim because of some large piece of machinery. I'm not so used to her being subject to time. The way the rest of us are.

Still, I sit in her room now, and I don't try to huddle in the farthest corner. I don't try to avoid looking at her or hearing her heart monitor and BP machines beeping like a metronome.

"What's good, Moms?" I say, so quiet I'm not even sure I managed to verbalize the words out loud. "You look nice today. Got a little flower in your hair and everything. Looks like your nurse might have even done a little blush or something."

I pull my faraway chair closer to her bed.

"I like that they're taking care of you in here. I sometimes wonder if I should have more input on your care. Theo refuses to let me take over as your proxy. He's such an asshole, Mom. Eventually I will, though. But for now, it's looking like you're doing okay."

There's a stray piece of lint on her shoulder—really, I swear there is—and I reach up to pick it away and then smooth out the fabric.

"I'm not exactly batting a thousand over here myself, so maybe I could stand to take some notes from you. I'm almost certain my boyfriend broke up with me. I've been in love with him since I was in, like, seventh or eighth grade. I'm gay, by the way. Did you know I'm gay? Never did get the chance to come out to you the way I did with Uncle Miles and Titi n'em. I miss him to distraction, that boy. Turns out that post-breakup, can't-eat, can't-sleep stuff is real."

I've tried so hard not to think about him, but he's there at every turn. I can find him in everything. When he was mine, that was a good thing. Felt like what Moms would have called *a blessing*.

Knowing Gabriel, seeing the ways he's still London but has

become Gabe, my Gabe, feels like watching a year go by at light speed. I like to think he and I loved like the seasons changed for us, and there is some truth to it.

Spring is when we decided that growing among the garden just wasn't for us and so we went off, a couple of middle-schoolers, and did our own thing. When summer arrived, we chose to cut out our hearts and freeze them for next year because we knew it'd mean limited hours together. When winter arrived, we never looked twice, jumped in the pools with all our clothes on and, eyes holding each other's, held our breath even after we'd come up for air. When autumn came for us, we redefined what it meant to watch leaves lose their colors, both of us changing, voices deepening and jaw lines sharpening little by little.

I like thinking that we loved like the seasons changed for nothing, because we were everything that couldn't exist during the little showers of rain that didn't get along with the sparks lit between us—and yet, still we did.

We loved like the seasons changed for us, but love can be so damn backward sometimes. It was never meant to hold any true singular definition. I've kind of realized, too, that once you've had a taste, you're sort of screwed, but it's okay.

Love is love is love is love, and I'm holding tighter than I should to the fact that we'll figure it out.

I exhale, growling because I'm so damn frustrated. "I don't know what I'm doing anymore. Or why I'm doing it. I just want to prove I'm worthwhile to someone and even though Uncle

Miles isn't around to see it or reap any of the benefits, I don't know how to let go of the fact that I owe him. That doing right by him would somehow make me right."

The drapes are only partially open, so I get up and open them wide. She has a great view. Or, the room has a great view. Moms isn't getting the opportunity to see it.

I walk back over to her, crouch down on my haunches, and whisper, "Would you hate me if I let it all go?"

I kiss her papery cheek before I go.

You know, I read online somewhere that there's so much discourse about the "beauty," or the lack thereof, of Van Gogh's *Sunflowers* that many critics don't even believe he painted it himself. That is, I think, how I want to feel.

I want to paint some ugly shit for me. The metaphor sucks, but the sentiment is still definitely a thing.

Man, he must have been so happy, painting those sunflowers. Sometimes all I want is a whole field of that feeling. A whole field of sunflowers.

The morning of the protest, that's the thing I'm thinking of when it happens. I feel like I'll always remember where I was—

in the room I share with Desh. What I was doing—packing everything I thought I *might* need into my backpack. Ready to move mountains and face the consequences. What I was thinking about the day I lost everything—sunflowers. Sunflowers sunflowers protest sunflowers.

I'm eighteen years old and I've come to realize that all the conversations that I've been in surrounding gentrification are hollow because there aren't many of us who understand what effective, considerate, quality services should look like in neighborhoods that house underrepresented populations.

That was a lot. I know.

There are no figurative neurological pathways that spell out exactly how we enhance those neighborhoods without displacing the people who make it worth everything.

That's the issue. So many times, I and many others have called the cupcake shops, Whole Foods, and juiceries the problem. Have targeted and boycotted them as if they are the issue, when really the root of it all is just that it's impossible for those of us in the neighborhood to afford them. And so, therein, I hope, should lie the solution.

It's just not that simple, though. It's really not. Otherwise, I think someone a lot smarter than me would have fixed it already.

But I'd like to think I'm on to something. I'd like to think I can step in one day and hold out my hand and offer the hood some real answers. Some real financial solutions that'll include a boost to our quality of life.

I don't want my kids to grow up and one day drown in Poverty PTSD the way I am. I'm sure as hell clawing my way up and out, but it's work. It's energy I could have been putting into my education. Into bettering my own personal world.

Do you see where I'm going with you? Start from the beginning of this chapter.

Read it again.

Good?

Yeah.

Now you're thinking. It's systemic oppression.

That's where the seed of problems that infect these neighborhoods comes from. And I want to fix it.

There's a Welsh word, hiraeth, that translates loosely to "homesickness." Thing is, the word is so much bigger than that. It's a longing, a visceral break in the heart that stems from losing a piece of the place you can't ever go back to.

Hiraeth. I like this word.

It's exactly how I feel about the apiary. Which is why, even though it's been seized, even though a crater opened up in my chest the moment it happened, we're still going to throw down. We have a point to make and goddammit, I'm not going to forego that chance.

The auction is being held in the early hours of the weekend.

Emery all but stitches herself to my back. "You're driving," she says, tossing her keys at me. She's through the student parking lot and sliding into her passenger seat a second and a half later.

"Emery," I say. And I stop there, because what else *can* you say? When did this stranger become my friend? When did "I don't know you" turn into "I love you"? The change must have crept in while none of us were watching. It's been like that with all my friends here.

The family Aunt Lisa was talking about.

I start the car.

Buckle up.

Signal.

Pull into traffic.

I feel okay.

feel okay until we are seated. The drive back to this particular part of Los Angeles, the affluent, never-seen-an-upheaval part of the city, is louder than I expect. It's louder in different ways than Baldwin Hills.

I hate that this loud feels fresher. Organic.

In the hood, your loud is ephemeral. It always feels like you're bleeding out instead of winning whatever battle is surrounding you.

The auction is located in the "conservatory" section of a local park. This part is quiet. It's all children's giggles and moms in yoga pants helping their stroller-strapped baby take a sip off a large bottle of kombucha.

Look, nothing against kombucha. I fucks with it.

But the point is, it's foreign. Also, stop giving your babies this organic crap and let their tiny bodies figure it out the way they're meant to, like, damn.

Here, I feel like I should be running. *We should not have come.* I readjust for the fiftieth time in my gray foldout chair, Em's hand in mine, making eye contact with each of the people in this far-too-crowded space. I wonder who will put a numeric price on the part of my soul that's up for sale today.

Is it irrational for me to fucking *loathe* the people of color sitting in this room with numbered paddles in their hands, ready to buy up some property that probably was built on the backs of less-affluent people just like them? It feels like a betrayal. Only, like, two-thirds of the room is white.

The rest, I don't even know how to process that.

A third—maybe the fourth?—scan around the room reveals Rick the Dick, sitting as close to the exit as one can get, as though he's got reason to run and wants to be prepared.

I inhale and exhale repeatedly to slow down the nausea that's resting at the bottom of my throat. Ever smelled the inside of an old book that's spent too much time not being read? Its pages shut long enough that it becomes something altogether different?

Some people enjoy that smell, get all kinds of dreamy eyed and nostalgic about it. I don't.

Funny, then, that the inside of this building smells exactly like that.

The old dude at the podium starts shouting out specifics on properties like his life depends on the heavy boom of his *"SOLD!"* declaration, spit flying from his mouth, nailing the front row with a little DNA. They fucking deserve it.

He's going and going, voice growing hoarser by the minute. And then my lot is up. Our lot, where my bees used to be, where I occasionally slept when Moms got too bad and then later when Theo did. Where I came out to Uncle Miles and he smiled because Black men aren't supposed to have words for that.

It's where I, like bees, learned to trust.

I am a glass house right now.

Emery presses her face into my shoulder and cups my cheek on the other side. "It's okay, Torr. It's okay. Just breathe."

The bidding starts just as a guy slides into the empty chair next to me.

Although he's heavy and armed with a deep-brown cane, he's also tall and moves like his bones have never known any kind of worry. He wears a vest, horn-rimmed glasses, and some kind of weight in his eyes that belongs to who only knows.

He pats my knee with a rough mallet of a hand. "It's gon' be alright, son."

The bass rumble of his voice is soothing. Comforting. Kind of like aloe on a burn. Or Vicks on the bottoms of your feet when you're sick. Thank you, Aunt Lisa.

"What's your name, now, son. Tell me what your name is," he says.

I push past the tears that have settled on the rims of my eyes. "Torrey. It's Torrey."

He nods. "Good name. And your girl here. The one tryin' just so hard to save you. Who's she?"

"She," Em says, a smile in her voice, "is called Emery."

"Ahh," the man says. "An excellent name."

"Can we ask your name, sir?" Emery whispers just as the auctioneer screams *"to the woman in the large hat!"*

"Well, you've gone and done just that, now, haven't you? My name's Miles Myrie."

I'm caught up in orbit and every piece of shrapnel that's been trapped inside me reaches out to the magnet that's in his words.

His name is Miles.

"Ain't that something?" he says on a laugh. "Miles Myrie. Mama was with them Jehovah's Witnesses when she decided to try and make my name into a big thing the wind would write down every time someone said it."

I glance up at him, meet his eyes, and shake my head.

Nothing. There's nothing there. I feel like I'm missing some kind of denouement. *His name is Miles.* Isn't that supposed to be the moment he stands up and buys my property for me and fixes whatever horrible fistfight has been happening in my chest for the past few hours?

But there's nothing in his eyes that says he knows me top to bottom. That says he loves me through nothing, anything, everything. Uncle Miles is not in there.

I look away.

"You know," he says. "I don't ever come here trying to buy nothing. Don't make no sense to me the way these people making money, entertainment, and hobbies off breaking people down."

"So, why are you here?" Em asks. I think she knows I'm incapable of anything resembling speech right now.

Mr. Myrie laughs.

I cannot refer to him as *Miles* right now. I won't.

His laugh isn't big like you'd expect. It's silent. You can tell it wants to get out, just wants to escape, just a little, so badly. But he holds it in. It is his and his alone.

"I come here—to things like this—to know what I'm up against," he says, solemn.

"Do you have a business up there on the hill? Own some property?"

Mr. Myrie nods. "Several. Most of the apartment buildings I occupy make it impossible for these people to ruin things completely. Out here talking about rent increases and tax increases and things that don't do nobody but white men no good."

"We've got a counter from number eight again. Going once!" the auctioneer says, and I can't breathe. Someone's made a final bid.

Mr. Myrie continues. "I tell my tenants one thing."

"Going twice!"

Who is it? Who has my heart in their hands right now?

"Nothing beats a failure but a try. Hang tight to that one, now, I tell you. *Oohwee.* Two Black kids like y'all? Yeah. Hang real tight to the try."

"SOOOOOLD TO NUMBER EIGHT. CONGRATULA-TIONS, SIR."

I do it. I change a glance up and search the room for paddle number eight.

It's Mathew. There's no kind of gravity on Earth or anywhere else that can hold my soul in place right now. Couldn't it have been anyone but him? Anyone but this man, this product of a system meant to break me.

I turn in Emery's arms, say—probably too loud—"Get me out of here, please, please. I have to get out of here."

And the world falls away as she all but lifts me and starts walking out of what can only be called hell on Earth, and when she realizes I'm hyperventilating, she presses my hand to her chest, right over her heartbeat.

Hang tight to the try.

33.

Ever walk past a random group of girls—could be at a school or a basketball game or a mall or a track meet or wherever—and just know which has things figured the hell out?

All four of my CAKE girls have this life thing on lock. I mean, I think I knew that, but it becomes abundantly clear when I get the text from Auburn that she, Clarke and Kennedy (along with Desh) have just reached the apiary after their six-hour drive from school.

It occurs to me again when, as Emery and I are walking up the street to the apiary, the others walk straight toward us sure—like the roads belong to them. Like they know they were born with a fight waiting for them and they've already strong-armed anyone or anything standing in their way.

I've been a longtime fan of Black women as the people who, as Malcolm X said, are the most disrespected people in the world—and yet they still run circles around us all.

Malcolm X had a lot of things right.

And they're all here, waiting for us when we finally arrive, members of the Collective, neighbors of the community, local business owners, Aunt Lisa, and—yes, even Mrs. Xu and Mr. Jones. They've brought ice packs, like, a dozen large aluminum trays of hot food from Daddy Mojo's, and cases on cases of bottled water.

You say "this is a protest," and the hood automatically thinks it's block-party barbecue.

Still, considering where I found myself when I came to get signatures of support, this feels like a really solid show of support.

Emery gets on her soapbox (yes, we actually gave her a literal soapbox to scream at people from; apparently, we are the people who just like to watch the world burn) and give everyone instructions.

"We don't want to stray too far from the apiary. The point of having this be home base is that it was technically private property and owned by Torrey. That's changed now, and we're here to let them know how we feel about it.

"So, while you can make your way up and down the block, let's try not to swing too far beyond that. And I know some of y'all headass dweebs from TC might think that doesn't apply to you—it does. Let's be mindful of where we are, and what we look like, how our melanin doesn't exactly serve us here. If there is a police presence, do not resist, do not fight back, comply and stay silent. We have half a dozen pro bono lawyers on reserve to deal with whatever may come. That applies to all protesting. Not just TC. Be safe. Be smart." She's silent for a moment, breathing hard. Then, on a yell, "Whose city?"

And we, as a crowd, a community, unbroken, yell, "Our city!"

It feels solid. Feels good.

It feels better when I turn to find him right beside me.

"What are you doing here?" I say.

The first thing I notice is the dark circles. They look like mine. His are cuter, though. Then I notice his outfit. He always did dress like the Afro-Latino version of Jamal Lyon. Beanie. Loose, incredibly chest-exposed thin tee. Cardigan thicker than Beyoncé.

He looks good. Comfortable. At home in his skin. But also, he looks tired. He looks like heartbreak.

He moves slowly, like he's not in control of his own feet, pushing straight into my arms. Or maybe it's me. Maybe I'm the one that brings our bodies flush against each other.

"I'm sorry," he says.

Damn damn damn. *Don't cry, don't cry, don't cry.*

I am. I'm crying. "Thank you, thank you, thank you for being here. With me."

"I didn't know," he says, a rush of words. "I did some research on bees. On their stats. On this farm, in particular."

"Why? Why would you do that?"

He pulls back, looks at me, and shakes his head. "Don't you know by now, príncipe? It's important to you. So it's important to me. Because *you* are important to me. All of you, exactly as you are. And listen. I found an apiary that's just thirty minutes outside of San Francisco."

I don't know where he's going with this. "Mm-hmm."

"The Addie Rose Apiary. They are willing to buy everything. Every hive and colony and most of your supply and stock. They'll even take care of transport."

"You . . . talked to them?" I ask.

"Yeah! That's what I'm trying to tell you. All you'd have to do is sign on the dotted line, pretty much."

Just a signature. Maybe I could even have Ryan Q look over the legal documents. Though, I'm not even sure that'd be necessary.

I'm familiar with the farm.

The Addie Rose Apiary is located not far from campus. It's in a better area for bee farming than the hot, smoke-heavy city air of Los Angeles. It's a really nice place. We've been up a few times to tour, Uncle Miles and I, and they've come down to see us a few times, too.

Bob and Elaine Rose are the softest, kindest, most Precious Moments type of old white people, and it's really hard not to beg them to adopt me at each visit.

They love bees.

They know bees.

They'll be very well taken care of.

"I was such a jackass to you," I say to Gabe. I can't believe he did all this.

"You weren't. I get it, okay? I hope that you understand, that now, *I understand.* Miles is important to you. And I also hope that with your bees moved, maybe a little of him can still live on. In a different way than we thought, but still somehow existing."

JFC. Like hot water poured into a pool of cold, the warmth in my chest starts right there in the middle and only spreads bigger and bigger, in ripples, out of me. I'm so happy. My heart is such an asshole. Everything hurts. Because this is the kind of bending no one has ever done for me. Nothing hurts. I know, right then, that he'd promise me the moon and break it in two if it meant I'd smile for even just a moment. That's who London Gabriél Silva is.

I exhale. "I am such a complete bonehead. I want you as you are. Would never ask you to change a single thing about you." I lower my voice to a whisper. A whisper in this big, public place. "My dancing, magical boy with his heart perpetually open and exposed."

"For you. Only for you, though, Torrey McKenzie. I'm going to stop running. You're right. I've lived this sort of free-floating life, and I can absolutely afford to come back down to Earth every now and again."

He would be the most beautiful Icarus, I think. Dancing a

little too closely to the sun all his life.

Gabe presses a kiss to the corner of my mouth just seconds before Desh walks up and grabs us both up into the most annoying hug and then walks away.

Low-key though, it feels amazing. Do not tell Desh I said so.

I laugh and lace my fingers on top of my head. "You did all this. You did all this, and I don't deserve you."

"Shut up," he says, a kiss pressed gently to my lips. A dragging, pulling thing.

Gabriel finds me again after what seemed to be a lengthy conversation with Mr. Jones. Weird and unexpected, I know. If anyone could have managed to get Mr. Jones talking, it's Gabe.

"I like him," Gabe says.

I glance back at Mr. Jones, whose eyes catch mine. His face is that same old frown, all bottom lip.

"Yeah, he likes you, too."

Mrs. Xu walks up and hands him a WE WILL VOTE YOU OUT poster. I try not to look too hard but he grabs it reluctantly and doesn't even put it down when she walks away to push food into the hands of a few people from the Collective.

Gabe laughs, not understanding. "You seem nervous."

"Do I?" I say. I'm not even sure he can hear me over the din that's inhabiting the neighborhood, bodies dodging around one another, familiar faces finding one another from across the street.

Across the way, my cousins Rhyan and Parris and a half dozen kids, probably a year or so younger than me, stand in a semicircle, freestyling. They're all wearing grey sweatpants and Jordans, which seems like the official uniform of protest.

"Yes. Estás bem?"

I lift my shoulders, ready to deny it. But why? Why should I? "Gabriel. Are we making a mistake? Protesting like this?"

"Oh, príncipe," he says. "This is not a mistake. Discussions, dialogue, policy proposals—they wouldn't listen to us."

I nod, but that's not enough for him, so he continues. "You know, Pac said once, in this interview, that the music he made was made that way for a reason. Black people started out with a basic request for equality and civility. We even said 'please.' And we got denied. So we made another request. That time, we didn't say please, and we also got just a little bit louder in volume. So after so many attempts at showing them the kind of civility we wanted given to us, we stopped worrying about respectability politics and words like *civility*. So now our requests for what are essentially our constitutional rights don't come with inside voices and the word *please*. Now we raise our fucking voices and scream ourselves hoarse and we demand, and we are not polite about it. All this to say, príncipe—are you listening?"

He takes my hand, squeezes, and goes on, "All this to say that you're doing the right thing."

I look down, but he doesn't let me get away with it. A finger under my chin, he meets my stare and says, "Look around. You're doing the right thing."

After a second or so, I catch Aunt Lisa's gaze and she smiles, winks, then turns back to Mrs. Jericho.

These individuals who've lived, loved, and worked in this neighborhood all their lives, these people who care so much it hurts them, these scorched-earth young activists—they're all here. Ready. Sure.

I owe them the same.

Issa protest, y'all.

And, goddamnit, do we ever. The farm is out of my hands now, gone and out of my control. But this? This is well within my control. Using who I am to demand something so basic as the preservation of life—that I can do. This protest is a message. It still has purpose.

Some buy T-shirts and others sign clipboards. A single mother of four children speaks to those who need bolstering, giving them her story, having won several court battles against her landlord who has been hellbent on trying to raise the rent on her eastside apartment building.

When the police do show, and the skin on the back of my neck prickles, we hold. They use the loudspeakers to "advise" us to stand down and go home.

We're having none of that. The marching band from Roosevelt, a local high school, uses their saxophones, violins, trombones, and trumpets like weapons to drown out their unwelcome warnings.

I've known all along that the only thing that'd really halt gentrifiers is intimidation.

The only thing that works is fear, Torrey. The fear of harm. So we got to take small steps, little by little, and show them that same thing. Because they are harming us.

Uncle Miles told me I wouldn't understand it when I was a kid. That someday, I'd be a man and then it might make more sense.

He was right.

Our ranks are small, and the tactics we've chosen to employ at this protest will be called controversial, even within the communities we're defending. But as young millennials of color, on fire for something bigger than ourselves, anxious over our economic standings in this country, I feel like we're onto something. A newer, more militant war on gentrification.

I don't bother trying to stay the night in the city. After a high like today, it's just not where I want to be. There's a better spot for my heart to hang out these days, and I'm going to take advantage of it.

Found families and all that.

I do run by there real quick though, once things have calmed and we've put our picket signs into the apiary's freshest earth with wooden posts. There are a few things I want to get out of my room at Theo's. Some pictures of me and Moms. I still have a couple of her favorite perfume bottles. Might be nice to have those things. You know, for when things maybe get a little rough, as life is wont to do.

It's supposed to be an in-and-out procedure, so while CAKE and Desh drive back to San Francisco, Gabriel decides to come with me, and we decide we'll catch the Amtrak later.

I should have known. I really should have known better.

Theo's seated on the living-room couch when I let myself in using the spare key. When I moved out, Theo made me leave my key.

He's not shocked when I come inside, but I sure as hell am. It's almost like he was waiting for me. He never hangs inside unless it's in his cave of a bedroom. Those are his two options: bedroom cave or in the back, surrounded by dying plants and grass that the LA sun just couldn't bother to have any mercy on.

"Heard your little party was a big hit with all the best minds in the city."

He damn well knows it wasn't a party. That adjective tells it all. "Little." It's the way Black people talk about things they deem worthless. To minimize them in stature. Toxic AF.

He's also not serious about that "best minds in the city" thing. He doesn't think anything about the hood is of value anymore—the apiary included. He moved here to live white adjacent, and when the neighborhood deteriorated in the early '80s, so did Theo's respect for the place he lives.

"Yeah," I say, walking past him. Just in and out. In and out, Torr.

I hurry up the stairs, around the banister, and into my room.

The one all the way in the back. It's mostly empty. Emptier than I remember leaving it when I left for college or even the last time I was here with Emery. It would not at all shock me if Theo was coming in here to throw away my crap when I'm not around, just to be a spiteful POS.

I grab the small box under my bed where the two perfumes are nestled into newspapers that should have long since been turned into something else, and next to it is a thick photo album. There are photos of Moms and me, Uncle Miles and me, the three of us together. Even a good dozen with Aunt Lisa in them.

That's all I need. I'm done. I hurry back down to my sweet boy with his rakish smile, all white teeth and strong jaw.

Just as I'm walking out the door, Theo, half asleep, calls, "What you taking out here? Don't think you can come up in here and take things that ain't yours, boy."

"None of what I have or want is yours, Theo." I turn to go again. In and out. Just in and out.

"It ain't gon' work," he laughs. "Whatever y'all was doing today for that farm ain't getting nobody nowhere. Watch."

"Okay," I mutter. "Whatever."

Theo laughs again. "Little girl just running away. Always running."

That stops me. It's been . . . a day. A bit of a day. And, so, I'm not prepared to put up with Theo's toxic-ass Black man homophobia. I'm so sick of this shit. I'm not doing it with him anymore. I'm done letting it happen.

"What the hell is the matter with you."

He sits up, the motion so much smoother than I've seen him move in a long time. "I'm all you got, you know that."

It's not true. I'm all he's got.

He goes on. "I'm all you got, and you don't want no part of me. How's that for some kinda family?"

I try to speak again, but he cuts me off. "You need to be done with me here. I can't stand looking at you no more, I'll be dead before I ever understand what this style of life is doing for you." He shakes his head. "You were raised better than this. I know it's bad parenting that got you here."

Bad parent—what? Bad parenting made me gay? News to me.

"I thought I'd intervened soon enough. I'll never understand, so what the hell's the gotdamn point." He's quiet. And I think he's done. And I'm trying to catch up to wherever he's at. But then he says, "The way you live, this disgusting life you're out here living . . ." He is this close to spitting at me. "It would break your uncle's heart—"

"He knew," I say. "He'd known for years."

He is so quiet. So quiet and still. I worry for the first time in my life whether Theo is going to hit me hard enough to do irreparable damage. I didn't think before I said that. I definitely should have thought before saying that. He's a tempest. A mildly contained brush fire. A titan ready to be loosed. And just when I think to speak again or even raise my arms to protect whatever part of me he can hurt the most, he says, as all the oxygen in the room stills, "Get out."

And I don't hesitate. I take my box and my photos and I get out. The door is closed and I'm halfway across the street, close, so, so close to Gabriel's arms, when I hear Theo scream, the rage of a wounded animal, "Don't ever come back!"

It's the sound of branches breaking under my feet.

I see my heartbreak mirrored in Gabriel's eyes.

I feel it in the way he reaches for me and pulls me into his arms. "I'll keep you safe," he whispers. "We'll shove this darkness into a box, and I'll keep you safe."

Violence is the first way Theopolis James McKenzie learned to hold anything. It's then that I know I'll do as he says. I won't ever, ever, come back to this place.

I was here.

It kind of makes sense why people feel the need to write that phrase on yellowing public-bathroom stall doors, high school yearbooks, and chalkboard walls in those hipster juice bars.

I want to leave my mark so everyone will know I was here. That, if I'm being honest, is also part of why I'm hanging on to the apiary with my claws sunk deep.

But maybe, it hits me, I need to find out what my bathroom stall door should be. Yes, this, too, is an awful metaphor. Take a shot every time I fire off a completely ridiculous analogy.

RIP your liver.

Point is . . . when I think about each of my friends, I see them having things they can call their own. CAKE has STEM— Kennedy's even branching out to art history—Gabe has ballet, Desh has photography. Desh is one of those annoying people who will completely interrupt the flow of walking traffic to lie on the ground to "get the shot." And me? I had a torrid love affair with my dead uncle's bee farm. Not great on a resume. Probably.

I'm heading down to meet Coco, but when I get there, there's a dude in one of the chairs at the table with her. My chair's there, my coffee in the spot she always puts it in. When I sit, it takes a moment for either to put their respective papers down and look at me.

"Hi?" I say.

"¿Qué pasa? Si quieres una página . . ."

Coco almost never speaks to me in Spanish. But when she does, she always does it twelve times faster than any non-Spanish speaker could hope to comprehend. She's patient with me though and has been working to slow it down a bit. And I've been teaching her about bees and honey harvesting. It feels like a pretty even trade.

"Yes, please. Who are you?" I say to homedude.

The guy laughs. He sounds like he's swallowed a cup of gravel someone lit on fire first. Descriptive, I know. He looks like Jeff Goldblum, though, so. You're welcome for that.

"I'm Dr. Ismael Palafox. I'm chair of the Agriculture Sciences department."

"Okay," I say. "Why are you here?"

Dr. Palafox turns to Coco. "Kid's kind of proprietary, isn't he, Coco?"

She shrugs. "I like him. He's a smart cookie. Torrey is my research assistant."

"I am?"

She ignores me. "Plus, he's pretty good about punctuality, so he can be whatever the hell he wants, cabrón."

Dr. Palafox laughs again. He does that a lot. Everything is always funny to white men, I've noticed.

"I'm here because Coco invited me. She mentioned your farm. I'm sorry about what happened. I do some work myself in the field. I imagine your Coco thought I might learn a thing or two from you. I think she's probably right for once."

She turns to me. "He's just here to hold the boring sections of the paper that we don't want, Torrey." And then after a moment of giggling at something in the business section—????—she turns to me and says, "It pays shit money, but it's certainly something, and you can work around and in between your classes."

"I am her research assistant," I say. And I sip my coffee and read about the state of our country with two college professors, one of whom is my boss, I guess, which isn't a thing I ever imagined myself saying.

What a time to be alive.

Normalcy.

It's Gabriel's casual kisses that make me feel like the world is tilting and twirling but remind me that I am not. Or the way he says, "Behave, príncipe," when I make every move in any book ever written about how to seduce your boyfriend during study group.

It's those nights I stop on a foggy Bay Area curb and text Emery or Desh from inside the mouth of a streetlamp.

It's weekly FaceTime calls with Aunt Lisa, who—right now, in this very moment—looks at me with what I think is nervousness . . . or hesitation? Whatever it is, it's got pins in her shoulders, lacing them up to a beam above her head, the weight of an anvil concaving her chest.

Whatever it is, it worries me.

"Titi. You good?" I say.

"Yeah, yeah! Hi, b—op! I almost tripped over this damn . . . Hi, baby. I'm okay. I'm fine. You alright? Eating?"

"Yes." Same thing every week. SMH.

"Sleeping?"

"Yes."

"Lotioning up after showers?"

"Yes, Titi. My God."

"Uh-uh," she says holding up a finger to the camera. "Don't be out here trying to shame me for loving on you, especially once I'm moved all the way up to the Pacific Northwest and—"

"I'm sorry, what."

"Mm. Didn't quite finesse that little tidbit of news, did I?"

What the ever-loving fuck is she talking about? "What on Earth are you talking about?" Had to clean it up for her. She'd have me by the ear so fast.

I have to sit. I have to sit down. I do, I sit.

"I got a job offer. I'll be doing what I love."

Science. Science is taking her away from me. "Where at?"

"Seattle. So, not that far!" she rushes to add.

"Seattle?"

"I'm sorry, Torr. I just applied without really thinking I'd get it. I've known I got it for a little while now, but they're giving me time to pack the house. And I wanted to stay . . . for the apiary, you know? Just in case? But I can't live with him anymore, you know that. I've been here too long anyway and the job, baby, it's perfect. They're relocating me. Putting me up in a bomb-ass apartment."

Jesus. "No way?"

"Deadass. And I mean, there's a spare room. I've been boxing up the rest of the things in your room and getting them all in storage until they decide to start shipping our belongings."

It's starting to rain. Sky's been at it all week.

Not the angry kind from this morning, the sad and tired type of rain that traces down the panes of tea shops and bookstores, half-assed and silly. Why is it that even silly rain transports me to nights I'd rather forget?

It rained the night we all rushed to Cedars to find out if Uncle Miles was okay, and it rained still when they told us he wasn't.

It rained the morning we came up to get Moms settled in her care center and stopped, then started again, a little fickle, as we made our drive back home.

It rained the day Gabriel left, all those years ago.

This rain—it does feel different though.

Or maybe *I'm* just different. Who knows.

To Aunt Lisa, I say, "You're all I have."

"I'm not. You know that. I've seen that. You've got a whole family unit up there. And when the semesters end and the holidays come, you come up to Seattle. You come home, to me."

"Okay," I say.

"Okay?"

"Yeah. Yes. Okay."

Maybe this won't be one of those times I have to remember rain for, the day Aunt Lisa left, promised to keep a spot in her heart for me, while fog and faith and raindrops all mixed with my tears.

Maybe Moms and Uncle Miles didn't leave us to Theo. Maybe they left us to each other.

That morning I walk into Coco's office and ask her for a favor. The next morning, Coco and I sit down at our usual coffee table. Soon, Dr. Palafox, the agrisci department chair, joins us.

He has, I don't know, maybe a minute of silence before I open my mouth and say exactly the attack Coco and I planned. "I want to declare my major, Dr. Palafox."

He looks up from the little dribble of coffee that he's just stained his Lacoste polo with. "Oh? And as of now, your major is?"

"Undecided," both Coco and I say simultaneously.

And I continue, "I'd like to change my major and for you to be my mentor."

"Mm," he says. "I see."

Coco rolls her neck when she says, "Cut the shit, Foxy. Sé lo que quieres."

We don't *actually* know he'd want me as his mentee. But Coco says he's always looking for some student to jump into eco projects with and junk.

He doesn't call our bluff. "Well. Alright then," he says.

Coco and I glance at each other, nod soberly, and continue to drink our coffee while trading sections of the newspaper.

Change.

The apiary, the bees, and the way it existed in a neighborhood made entirely of broken-up gravel—that's the reason I'm declaring my major. That's the reason I want to give myself to a cause I can institute some change in. In the grand scheme of things, I may be just a blip, a baby. But I've been on this road now for a while, feeling a thousand years older than what I've been told by every part of my past. Up until now, I'd been water coasting in at low tide. Now, I know I want to be—I know *I can be*—a tidal wave.

EPILOGUE

This is the end.

Here's what I've got for you.

I thought I could keep Uncle Miles alive forever. I thought I could keep the neighborhood the same forever, thought I could still exist as part of it forever even though the relationship was parasitic as hell.

Sometimes we make decisions that we think are best for us, when it's clear they aren't. We do things that will make us feel better. Most of the time, they don't. You got any moments in life like that?

Afraid of a future with choices in it, I acted on feelings that had no right to be there. Guilt, eating me alive because Miles is gone. And I'm here. Living. In love. Changing things.

I tried to hang on to him forever, c/o a farm with some bees in it.

But forever doesn't exist as a solid, measurable thing, y'know?

I'll paint you a picture—in the abstract, it lives in the backseat of orange buses and in the denim lining of Uncle Miles's shirt that smells like Indica.

When the movie ends, there is nothing left but credits and darkness, right? Forever is impossible, like those Barbie dolls I used to get my ass kicked for playing with, the Mattel-brand flavor of imperfection still on my taste buds.

I guess one day I'll learn to wake up and embrace each moment. It'd be great if they didn't pass by so quickly though. That's what I got from the farm, from the Hill. Moments. Change. The traffic of it leaves skid marks of longing across my highway heart. That's all it'll ever offer me, and you know what, *that's fine.*

Today, forever will exist in the span of a second, right when Gabriel's soft lips meet mine and his smile breaks right up against my mouth, triggering my own need to smile with every part of me. When that moment becomes forever, and I'll know that is what eternity looks like when it's not wearing any masks, not cursing my name or sexuality, not pressuring me to fight a thing I am helpless to win.

Gabe's pretty much been my perpetual happiness. With him, this forever in me is naked for public viewing, and when it's like this, the world doesn't mind that for once I choose not to wear a frown.

THE END.

ACKNOWLEDGMENTS

H ooboy. Round 2.

 Bit of a doozy.

I can't believe I get to do this again, lol, who let me do this again??

Oh. Right.

People To Blame:

First, my editor, Ashley Hearn. Hi. This is your fault. I love you, thank you for being my friend, enabler, creative sounding board and coffee/beer educator. Twice.

My agent, Jim McCarthy aka Jimyoncé aka the Artemis to my Sailor Venus. Guys, if you ask Jim, he'll say he just sorta came in and tied some things up. But really he kind of saved me, The Author Me. Jim, your support has been . . . immense and stunning and just too perfect to comprehend. The greatest gift an author can receive and I'm so ready to hit the ground running (or, like, briskly walking—no more falls, pls!) with you. You are a sunflower in a field of dandelions, and they ain't ready for us.

Here's where you raise a glass and do shots in the name of Emery (tysm for the name!)/Zig, Dahlia/Fig, Cheyamma, Lily Mamas, Xtina & Lolo, Jay Elliot and Ryan. Without you guys, I'd have fallen long before this draft ever saw the light of day. Would've been out here pasty and pale and incomplete as heck at like 13k words.

Tehlór, you're always coming in clutch! Thanks, kid. And thank you for teaching me what "clutch" means. ilyok?

My Page Street/Macmillan editorial fambam, OMFG, GUYS. Lookit us! Out here! My publicists, Lizzy Mason and Lauren Cepero and my copyeditor, Rebecca Behrens, I'm still just a baby author when it comes to all this. You guys have provided me with the equivalent of juice boxes and Uncrustable sandwiches after school. My cover designer Laura Gallant, production editor Hayley Gundlach, Page Street's kick ass editorial assistants, Madeline Greenhalgh and Tamara Grasty, and interns Max Baker and Sabrina Kleckner—thank you so much for having ya girl's back. Lauren Knowles, to you I say, PINK DRINK!!!!! And to the Macmillan sales team—you lot are a fresh box of Krispy Kreme donuts wrapped in Christmas lights. Thank you for helping me tell stories that breakdown and interrogate the spaces where people like me have never been permitted.

My mamma Lynette (thank you for birthing me, sorry about those first 18 years), my dad "Brother Wesley" (for that Malcolm X poster in the garage) and siblings, Donnis (one artist to another, thanks for always reading my words), Pepper (thank you always for opening my doors, carrying my heavy luggage to the car and making me breakfast), and Jew (for keeping me humble and making sure I always know where to go if rock bottom drops lower than rock bottom). But especially, Trishalish. Hi, Sissy. I FUCKIN' LOVE YOU! You already know. Mashallah, you're my everything.

Shouts out to Zoloft, Wellbutrin, and Xanax, the realest mothafuckin MVPs!

My KS (name giver!!! <3), Robert Montano, Ellie, Heather, Weston, Xen, Rikki Leigh, Regan, Darren, Cullen, Shay and Julie—you guys kept me laughing through the completion of this dumb heart-job. Thanks, bigly.

My teens (by now, newly minted college freshmen!!) at the volunteer rec center, thank you for early morning Cheerios and bagels with too many inside jokes but not much cream cheese. Thank you for letting me in and for letting me steal scenes from our early morning laugh riots for this book. And to Israel, who started as "the kid who just drinks orange juice," became my mentee, moved into being my friend, and ended up my little brother. Love you, buggy.

To my dance family—no words, just fucked up drunken fouettés.

To the city of Los Angeles. LOL oh man, I freakin' hate you. But also? You're a little bit irresistible.

On that note—shout out to Nipsey Hussle and all of Slauson. Rest in power, sunflower.

And to all those who read and loved *Home and Away*. Or those who read it and felt it was "ehh, ok, not worth 5 stars but still pretty good, 3.5 I guess"—random Goodreads reviewer.

Because every one of you counts. You're the reason I get to do this again. You're also to blame. *hard wink*

Who's up for round 3?

ABOUT THE AUTHOR

CANDICE MONTGOMERY is an LA transplant now residing in Seattle. By day, she writes YA lit about Black teens across all their intersections. By night, she teaches dance and works in The Tender Bar. Her debut *Home and Away* (Page Street, 2018) was named a *Kirkus Reviews* best YA novel of 2018.